A PUFFIN BOOK

PROPERTY OF

_____

_____

COLIN DANN was born in Richmond, Surrey, in 1943. After leaving school he worked for a textile company before his real love – the world of books – brought him a job in publishing in London. His first book, *The Animals of Farthing Wood*, was inspired by his love of wildlife and was published in 1979. It was an immediate success, winning the Arts Council of Great Britain's National Book Award for Children's Literature. Six sequels and a prequel have followed and in 1992 a major animation series appeared on BBC television.

In addition to the Farthing Wood books Colin has written many other animal stories, including a trilogy about a pride of African lions. He lives with his wife Susie in a converted Oast House on the Sussex/Kent border.

COLIN DANN

THE ANIMALS OF FARTHING WOOD
THE ADVENTURE BEGINS

Illustrated by Trevor Newton

A PUFFIN BOOK

PUFFIN BOOKS

UK | USA | Canada | Ireland | Australia
India | New Zealand | South Africa

Puffin Books is part of the Penguin Random House group of companies whose
addresses can be found at global.penguinrandomhouse.com.

puffinbooks.com

First published by Hutchinson Children's Books 1994
Reissued in this edition 2016
004

Text copyright © Colin Dann, 1994
Illustrations copyright © Trevor Newton, 1994

The moral right of the author and illustrator has been asserted

Set in 13.5/20.5 pt Sabon LT Std
Typeset by Jouve (UK), Milton Keynes
Printed and bound in Great Britain by Clays Ltd, Elcograf S.p.A.

A CIP catalogue record for this book is available from the British Library

ISBN: 978-0-141-36874-0

To Caroline Roberts
with much appreciation for many years of
enthusiastic support and advice

Contents

Preface

THE AIR was quite still. Starlight bathed the frosty ground with silver. The woodland seemed to be drowsing in the silence of a winter's night. A lean fox trotted noiselessly beneath the trees, seeking shelter before sunrise. A vixen's cry – one he recognized – caused him to halt suddenly, then change direction. He answered the cry with three short yaps.

The vixen was standing under a huge beech tree, her body pressed against its smooth grey trunk. She too was lean; leaner than the fox. She called again. The fox ran towards her.

'I need your help,' said the lean vixen. 'Just as before.'

'Good,' the lean fox replied. 'I'm glad you thought of me.'

'It's for a different reason this time,' the vixen said. 'Come and see.' She led him through the Wood to a clearing. In the clearing several animals were darting about, chasing one another playfully. These were otters. The foxes stood and watched them for a while.

'What's the problem?' Lean Fox asked.

'They are,' came the answer. 'The otters. This is *my* hunting territory. I've told them to leave, but they only mock me.'

Lean Fox turned to look at his companion. She was regarding him steadily; expectantly. He turned away again. 'They don't appear to be doing any harm,' he murmured.

'Of course they're doing harm,' Lean Vixen corrected him irritably. 'They're snapping up all the voles. What am *I* to eat?'

Lean Fox's eyes widened. 'Otters? Killing voles?' he queried in surprise. 'Why would they do that? They're fishing animals.'

'How do I know why?' the vixen barked. 'Because they're hungry, I suppose. I thought you'd be some help,' she added disappointedly.

'Well, I . . . ' Lean Fox began awkwardly. 'You know, otters are special creatures, aren't they?'

'Oh, not that old story again,' the vixen sighed. 'That's all we ever hear. Well, what am I to do then? Starve?'

'Isn't there anywhere else you can go? I mean, there are voles and mice throughout the Wood. Plenty for everyone.'

'It's difficult poaching another fox's territory,' Lean Vixen replied. 'Besides, what's to stop these precious otters scouring other areas once they've laid this one waste. They're lethal hunters. I've seen them in action.'

Lean Fox felt he had to do something. The vixen was relying on him. He trotted forward.

As he approached, the otters stopped gambolling for a moment and looked at him. They showed no fear.

'Why must you take our prey?' Lean Fox yapped boldly, aware the vixen's eyes were on him. 'Don't you have enough of your own?'

The largest otter, a mature adult and a sleek, healthy-looking animal, replied airily, 'No, we don't, although what business it is of yours I fail to see.'

Lean Fox's hackles rose. 'It's my business because voles are a fox's staple diet,' he growled.

'Really? How interesting,' the sleek otter answered sarcastically. 'Perhaps you'd better improve your hunting technique.'

The younger otters giggled in a kind of high-pitched whistle. Lean Fox tried to chase them away. They began to show off, tumbling and somersaulting and leaping around, but always keeping well out of his reach. The otters had a wonderfully fluid kind of agility. Lean Fox returned to the vixen's side.

'I don't think there's much I can do at present,' he muttered. 'They simply make me look foolish.'

'Something *will* have to be done,' Lean Vixen declared. 'Why should foxes give way to these . . . these . . . animal clowns?'

1. Otters Abroad

THERE had always been otters in Farthing Wood. They lived on the fringe of the woodland along the banks of the stream. There they made their homes and dived for fish and frogs and mussels. Over the years their numbers had steadily declined as the resources of the stream – and indeed the pond – had dwindled almost to exhaustion. But as long as there were otters, however few, Farthing Wood was safe and the site protected from development.

These otters enjoyed a special status because they were the only ones to be found over a wide area. Local wildlife groups had campaigned hard, and successfully, for their preservation. The otters knew they were special and they made sure all their neighbours knew it too. They were far from being the most popular of creatures. When they turned to hunting on land because of the shortage of aquatic prey, there was bound to be resentment.

The crucial decision had been taken by one of the most experienced females. She was a mother of three cubs, none of whom was getting enough to eat. One evening, instead of leading her youngsters out of their holt to the stream, she headed for the woodland. The cubs were puzzled.

'The water! Where's the water?' they chattered to each other.

'Hush,' their mother quietened them. 'Aren't you hungry? Of course you are. Well, we must try our luck elsewhere.'

The cubs began to treat the outing as an adventure. They bounced along behind their sleek mother, whistling excitedly. The darkness of the Wood, however, affected their high spirits. The cries of unfamiliar night creatures reached their ears. They fell silent. There was a rustle of dead leaves and Sleek Otter, the mother, pounced suddenly. The youngsters surrounded her. A vole dangled lifeless from her jaws. Sleek Otter dropped it amongst her cubs.

'The first of many,' she said. 'This wood's alive with prey.' She watched the cubs sniffing at the unusual food, unsure of its taste. 'You'll soon get used to it. You'll *have* to,' she added. Her rippling body bounded forward again.

The cubs juggled with the dead animal, tossing it from one to another. Finally one of them ate it, chewing the vole on one side of the mouth as with a fish.

'Good,' the cub whispered and smacked her lips. The three cubs rejoined the hunt.

Sleek Otter's expertise proved to be deadly to any mice, shrews or voles who were scurrying through the leaf litter that night. These little animals had accustomed themselves to the threat of foxes or stoats. But the swiftness and acrobatics of the otter party were something new to them. They didn't know how to escape these new hunters. All four of the otter family caught prey and their appetites were more than satisfied.

'Fish or no fish, we shan't starve,' cried Sleek Otter.

The cubs took up the chant. They felt pleased with themselves.

And this was when Lean Vixen, who was hunting that night too, first encountered them. Her astonishment at seeing her territory invaded by otters made her lose her own quarry and she went hungry.

'Clumsy fox,' shrilled the cubs. They had witnessed her bungled attack on a young rabbit which had managed to reach the safety of its burrow. Lean Vixen growled and she bared her teeth.

'Pay no attention to her,' scoffed Sleek Otter. 'She wouldn't dare to meddle with us.' The otters ran on, under the nose of the vixen who gaped after them. Moments later Sleek Otter killed a shrew without apparent effort, as if to emphasize her superiority. The cubs giggled with delight.

'We shan't starve,' they squealed. 'We shan't starve.'

Lean Vixen watched angrily as Sleek Otter's antics produced four more voles for her cubs to enjoy. The sight of the otter family gobbling up prey from her own preserve made the vixen very angry.

'Haven't you space enough to hunt around your den without stealing from me?' she barked.

As if by way of an answer, Sleek Otter snapped up a fieldmouse and ate it herself with elaborate pleasure. 'We're not stealing anything,' the mother otter retorted. 'The mice are here for any hunter to catch. It's not my fault you weren't skilful enough to catch them first.' She turned and called to her cubs. 'Come, youngsters. Let's go for a swim.' The otter family went on their way, chattering and laughing merrily.

Lean Vixen shivered in the cold night air. 'They'll be back,' she told herself. 'I need some support.'

Other otters joined the hunters in Farthing Wood as the winter progressed. They really had no choice. Fish large enough to satisfy their appetites were increasingly difficult to find. Frogs, their other mainstay, were in hibernation and would mostly be hidden until the spring. So the competing foxes, stoats and weasels began to suffer. They couldn't keep any part of the Wood for themselves. There seemed to be otters all over the place, seizing their quarry before their very eyes.

'You and me,' said Sly Stoat to Quick Weasel, 'are fools. Look at the way we're being cheated. And what do we do about it? Nothing. No wonder those otters are so scornful.'

'Don't you have a sneaking admiration for their ability?' Quick Weasel asked. 'Otters have such style. But you'd better talk to the foxes. *They're* in a very ugly mood.'

'Maybe,' Sly Stoat grunted, 'although they appear to me to be as hypnotized as you are by the whole display. If there's going to be trouble, I'll be on the side of the foxes. We ought to drive those slippery customers right back into the water where they came from.'

'You creatures are so envious, aren't you?' a voice said behind them. Smooth Otter, a big male, had heard every word. 'You ought to be grateful to us, all of you. We otters are the protectors of Farthing Wood. Why is the Wood untouched? Because of us. We're very special animals. Humans daren't meddle here. We're the only otter colony for miles around. So as long as we choose to live here with you, you're safe. Remember that!'

'How can we ever forget?' Sly Stoat complained. 'You never cease to ram it down our throats!'

'Stoat has a hasty temper,' Quick Weasel chipped in. She was a little scared of the dog otter who towered over them. 'He didn't mean everything he said.'

Smooth Otter laughed hollowly. 'I imagine not,' he grunted, staring fiercely at the stoat. Then typically, his mood changed and he began to dance around them playfully. 'Try and catch me,' he cried.

Sly Stoat turned away in disgust. 'I'd rather catch myself a meal if you've no objection,' he answered sourly.

The foxes were certainly planning to act. 'They overlook how vulnerable their young ones are,' Lean Vixen said. 'Just let me get hold of an otter cub! It'd be worth a whole clutch of voles. *I'm* not going to stand idle any longer,' she vowed.

mouthful or two. And then the otters began to taunt them.

'You're not in the same league,' Sleek Otter laughed as Lean Fox lost a fieldmouse he had been trailing to the otter's superior agility. 'You've no flair, you see. No wonder humans pay you no attention.'

'What do you mean?' snapped Lean Fox.

'Ask yourself. Why haven't the humans moved in here? They've done so everywhere else.' She paused to eat the mouse. 'You foxes,' she went on with her mouth irritatingly full, 'are common creatures like the weasels and stoats. Humans disregard you. They ruin your homes and habitats and build over the top of them. But not here. Why? Because of us. How fortunate you are to have us in your midst.'

'You can go *too* far,' Lean Fox snarled. 'I've heard threats. Watch out for your youngsters!'

'Pooh. You'd never catch us,' scoffed Sleek Otter. 'Just you try!' And the otter family raced away through the darkness in a looping sort of movement, the mother at the front and the cubs in a line behind, for all the world like a kind of serpent's tail.

Lean Vixen was plotting revenge. She knew roughly where the otters had their lairs and she wanted to teach them a lesson. She intended to strike at the cubs. When she knew the otter population was absorbed with its hunting she slipped along to the stream-side and, in the evening shadows, followed Sleek Otter's scent to a hollow tree that stood by the bank. Lean Vixen sniffed all around. A cold wind blew, ruffling her fur. She could see no entrance to the otter family's holt, but their scent was so strong she knew their den must be somewhere inside the hollow tree. Growling low in her throat, she decided to hide herself nearby and lie in wait for their return.

'You're in for a little surprise, my slick friends,' she muttered and chuckled at the thought, lying down amidst a tangle of dry rushes. Water lapped at the edges of the dead vegetation as the stream glided past. Lean Vixen waited patiently, ears cocked for the slightest sound of movement along the bank.

Nothing. Only the wind sighing in the leafless boughs of the Wood and the dry rasp of reed-stems around her. Lean Vixen yawned and shivered slightly. Suddenly upstream there was a series of splashes. The vixen turned her head. There was no sign on the dark water.

'A fish jumping,' she grunted.

But, beneath the surface of the stream, Sleek Otter and her three cubs were swimming silently to their holt entrance underwater. They pulled themselves, dripping, into their den inside the hollow willow and shook themselves vigorously. Lean Vixen heard the chatter of the cubs and sprang up in amazement. She ran to the tree. The otters' voices were unmistakable. They were safe inside their den and she had been outwitted. She snarled. The chattering ceased abruptly, then broke out again.

'Mother, I heard a fox!'

'So did I, so did I. It's outside.'

'Take no notice,' Sleek Otter answered them. 'Let it snoop. It'll gain nothing,' she added in a raised voice for the vixen's benefit.

Lean Vixen knew she was powerless and she spun round angrily. She looked at the stream, then back at the willow, and all at once she realized how the otters had bypassed her. She crept down the bank and peered closely at the icy water, leaning far over as she tried in vain to locate the otters' secret entrance. Moments later something bumped hard against her from behind and she was tipped forwards, plunging helplessly into the stream.

A whistling screech of laughter followed her fall. Lean Vixen recovered herself and, as she struggled to keep afloat, she recognized

Smooth Otter who was prancing gleefully on the bank. The dog otter had returned from hunting, had seen the prowler and had deliberately run into her, pitching Lean Vixen into the water. Now, as the vixen began to yap angrily, other otters arrived to taunt her.

'Fox in the water!' one cried. 'Can't seem to swim, can it?'

'Stiff as a piece of wood,' another answered. 'Doesn't move its body at all.'

'Isn't it slow, its legs hardly move,' commented a third.

'Small wonder it can't catch anything,' Smooth Otter laughed. 'It'd take all night to cross a field!'

Lean Vixen was seething. While she had no pretensions to being a skilful swimmer, she prided herself, like all foxes, on being speedy overland.

'You – you smarmy, conceited pu–pup–puppies!' she roared, kicking out furiously for the bank. She wanted to tear into them, bite them, snap at them, anything to vent her anger.

'Let's teach her to swim,' suggested Sleek Otter who had left her holt again to join in the fun. Her cubs dived and splashed around the vixen, spraying her with water and goading her all the more. The other otters hustled into the stream and Lean Vixen was surrounded by bobbing, dipping bodies that seemed to appear and disappear again in a bewildering variety of places. They jostled and pushed her away from the bank. Then they grasped her legs with their horribly sharp teeth and pulled her underwater, only releasing her when her lungs seemed about to burst.

'Get . . . away,' Lean Vixen gasped helplessly. 'Leave . . . me alone. Cowards, all . . . of you. Can't fight . . . fairly!' She battled to the bank but, just as she thought she was free, they surrounded her again and, shrieking with delight, butted her over on to her back. Lean

Vixen was almost too tired to resist. With a supreme effort she righted herself, scrabbled for a foothold on the bank and heaved herself clear. There was nothing to do now but run for it. Yet running was out of the question. She was exhausted, freezing cold and humiliated. Her legs smarted painfully where the otters' teeth had bitten. Blood flowed from the wounds. She drew several shuddering breaths whilst her tormentors leapt around her like demons.

'We don't like snoopers,' Sleek Otter shrilled. 'Tell that to the other foxes, in case they have any bright ideas.'

'Wasn't worth it, was it?' chanted another. 'You do look a mess!'

'You can't put one over on an otter!' cried Smooth Otter. 'We're supreme. Haven't I said so before? Now you've only made yourself look silly.'

'Run on home and dry off, I should,' Sleek Otter taunted.

'Dry off, dry off and clear off,' one of the cubs cried, and shrieked with laughter at the cleverness of his joke.

Lean Vixen slunk homewards, her pride and self-esteem battered. She avoided any of the other foxes and crept into her earth. Luckily Lean Fox was absent. For a long time she shivered miserably.

Gradually anger rekindled in her heart. Certainly the otters had bested her this time. She realized she had made an error of judgement. They were clever animals all right and she knew she should have used a more subtle approach.

'Conceited, vain buffoons,' she growled. 'I'm not finished yet. They won't be jeering next time. A bit of old-fashioned fox cunning is what's needed: the badger was right. There's more than one smart animal in Farthing Wood.'

3. No Playfellow

DURING the following days Lean Vixen racked her brains for a means of retaliation. She didn't mention her humbling experience with the otters to the other foxes. She hoped that none of the animals in Farthing Wood would learn how she had suffered, passing off her injuries as bramble scratches. And now the otters showed another side of their nature.

Snow had been falling intermittently for a day or two. The ground was covered throughout the Wood to a depth of a couple of centimetres.

It was an open invitation to the otters' playfulness. They made slides on the stream's banks and, one after another, the cubs tobogganed down them in the greatest glee, then returned for another go. Their mother didn't hesitate to join in. Up and down the length of the stream the otter community was playing, from the youngest to the oldest. They loved the snow and couldn't understand why the other Farthing Wood inhabitants appeared to be ignoring its possibilities for fun.

'Dreary lot, aren't they?' Smooth Otter remarked to a lone female. 'They need cheering up. Ought to be enjoying themselves on a lovely crisp day like this. Life can't be serious all the time.'

'What are you going to do?' asked the bitch otter. 'Most creatures are asleep in the daytime.'

'Seek some of them out,' he replied as he ran off. 'Why,' he cried, 'they don't know what they're missing.'

Under the trees Smooth Otter sought playmates amongst those who were, in other respects, rivals. This contradiction in roles didn't strike him. He was bent on a round of pleasure and he wanted others to be the same. Fresh prints in the snow led him to Sly Stoat's den. He bounded along boisterously, slipping and sliding on purpose in the powdery snow, calling all the while for others to join him.

A jay screeched at him from a lofty bough. 'Mad creature! Lost your wits?'

The otter skidded to a stop, somersaulted over and looked up, his head caked with lumps of snow. 'Wits? You don't need wits on a day such as this,' he cried. 'All you need is high spirits!'

The jay screeched again and flew off in alarm. Sly Stoat's head popped out of a burrow. 'Oh, it's you,' he said as he saw Smooth Otter. 'I might have guessed an otter would be causing the commotion.'

'Where's your sense of fun?' was the answer. 'Come on, I'll chase you through the snow.'

Sly Stoat's head disappeared at once.

'There's nothing to fear,' Smooth Otter assured him. 'It's only a bit of sport. Tell you what, you chase me. Set your blood tingling!' He raced away, expecting the smaller animal to follow. After a while he turned, but there was no sign of the stoat. 'Oh, what's the matter with them all?' Smooth Otter muttered. 'Where are –' He broke off as he saw a familiar figure padding softly, cautiously, across a glade. It was Stout Fox. 'Hallo, let's see how the land lies here,' the otter said to himself. 'All foxes aren't the same. Perhaps this fellow would enjoy a run.'

He gambolled across. Stout Fox was at once on his guard. His hackles rose and he bared his teeth.

'No call for that, Foxy,' Smooth Otter told him glibly. 'What's the problem?'

'What a question,' the fox growled. 'You otters are always a problem.'

'Let bygones be bygones,' the otter offered. 'I want your company.'

'Company? Whatever for?' Stout Fox asked suspiciously.

Smooth Otter explained.

'Snow? Play?' the fox repeated dully. 'I don't know what you're talking about. You otters are all crazy, but I've more sense than to listen to you. And I'll give you a spot of advice. Keep away from Farthing Wood if you value your safety.' He turned his back and continued on his way.

'Please yourself,' Smooth Otter called after him. 'You're the loser.' Setting his face once more in the direction of the stream, he mumbled, 'Better stick to my own kind. What's the use of courting others' friendship?'

Of course there were plenty of playfellows amongst the otters. But the antics of the otters that early morning had attracted interest, after all, outside their own group. Two delighted human onlookers were trying hard to keep still behind a thin screen of vegetation as they watched the animal gymnastics. Wildlife enthusiasts were not a rare sight in Farthing Wood. They came hoping chiefly for a glimpse of the otters whose existence was well known in the area. Usually these clever animals confined their activities to those times when people were absent from the Wood – during the night and around dawn – and so they were only occasionally spotted. Now their enjoyment of the snow drove caution to the winds. The two amateur naturalists couldn't believe their luck. It was as though the otters had put on a special display for them. And the humans were not the only witnesses.

'Just look at those show-offs,' Lean Vixen grumbled to Lean Fox as they stood together on the threshold of their new den. 'Running and sliding about like that, don't they ever grow up? They have no dignity.'

'I'm more concerned about the way they draw humans into our home,' Lean Fox answered. 'They're always bragging about the fascination they hold for humankind. And look, there are two of them now on the other side of the stream.'

Lean Vixen instinctively dropped to her belly. 'I never feel safe when they're about,' she murmured, half to herself. 'They can never be trusted. Come inside the den; let's get out of sight.'

Lean Fox followed her through the entrance to the dark interior.

'We ought to protest,' Lean Vixen complained to her mate. 'We don't want human intruders around when our cubs are born.'

'That's a long way off,' Lean Fox answered. 'But I agree. Otters are a constant nuisance these days. I'm concerned about the problem of food when we're bringing up our litter. We shall have to come to a sort of agreement with them before then.'

'Don't kid yourself,' Lean Vixen said sarcastically. 'The only kind of agreement they'd want is one on their own terms.'

The competition for prey heightened after some heavier snowfalls. Food became particularly difficult to find for every creature. There were thick layers of snow throughout the Wood. When prey did occasionally surface, there were tussles, not only between fox and otter, but fox and stoat, stoat and weasel. Every hunting animal was ravenous and they scuffled continuously. The foxes sometimes caught a rabbit unawares. Otters never attempted to hunt rabbits and so, except for the stoats, the foxes had a clear field. But rabbits were always quick to recognize danger and it was generally only old or sick ones that the foxes could reach.

As tension between the different groups reached its height, the otters stopped visiting the woodland. The foxes were first to notice.

'They've seen sense,' Stout Fox remarked, recalling his warning.

Lean Fox wasn't convinced. 'No,' he replied cautiously. 'It's not as simple as that. There's another explanation.'

It was Kindly Badger who provided it. He was digging holes in the snow nearby to get at acorns and roots. The foxes stopped to pass the news.

'Oh, hadn't you heard?' was the badger's reaction. 'The otters have fallen sick – at least, many of them have. Voles, mice – wrong diet, you see. Doesn't suit them. They should have kept to what they like – fish.'

'There you are,' Lean Fox said to his larger friend, 'it's not as simple as you thought.'

Stout Fox was irritated. 'Does it matter? As long as they leave the Wood alone . . .'

Kindly Badger looked from one to the other. 'It'll be of benefit to all of us, won't it? I mean, if they revert to fishing. Yet there was some question of a dearth of fish, so it's anyone's guess what the otters will try next.'

Quick Weasel was about to cross their path, but she saw the bigger animals in time and altered her route. 'She's a cunning one, isn't she, your mate?' she cried to Lean Fox from a safe distance.

He was puzzled. 'What do you mean?'

'She planned this. With the sly stoat. The otters are sick because the voles are sick. The vixen and stoat knew of a vole colony where most of the adults were ailing – some sort of infection, I believe – perhaps from a parasite. So they rounded up as many as they could and left them in the path of the otters, where they come from the stream.'

Stout Fox was impressed. 'Well, there's cunning for you,' he remarked. 'To think that she planned all that without your knowledge,' he added with a glance at Lean Fox.

Lean Fox looked uncomfortable. He had nothing to say. But Kindly Badger had.

'Cunning, maybe, but rash,' he commented. 'We can't afford any danger to the otter population. We depend on their thriving.'

'They'll survive; you can count on it,' was Stout Fox's opinion. 'At least they won't be so keen in future to raid our woodland larder.'

4. Changes

SOME of the otters looked unlikely to survive. Indeed the cubs were failing visibly. Sleek Otter was at her wits' end.

'What can I do?' she implored other adults. 'They can't move, they can't eat. They won't leave the holt. Their sad little cries haunt me day and night and they're growing weaker all the time. I can't bear to see the looks of anguish in their big weeping eyes.'

'Have you brought them a fish?' another female enquired. 'Healthy food is their only chance now.'

'I swam half the length of the stream yesterday to catch them something wholesome,' Sleek Otter replied. 'There wasn't enough for all of them. I brought some large mussels to the den, but the youngsters ignored them.'

'Have you consulted the smooth one?' asked the other female. 'He's been trying to help some of the sick adults.'

'No, but I'll do so,' Sleek Otter mumbled despairingly. 'I really don't think I've much time left.'

She knew where to find the big male, and trotted purposefully through the snow towards his holt. The otter slides were still visible on the banks of the stream but no animal played now. How things had changed, the otter mother thought to herself. It hardly seemed possible that her cubs had galloped up and down in such high spirits only a few days earlier.

'It's my fault,' she blamed herself. 'I didn't take sufficient care of what they ate. *I* wasn't raised on furry mice. How could I expect my young ones to benefit from them?' A little later she wailed shrilly, 'But they have to eat *something*. What was I to do?'

Smooth Otter greeted her gravely. Then he said, 'I can guess why you're here. I've told others and I'll tell you. We're all guilty of neglecting to take precautions.'

'Precautions? What precautions?' Sleek Otter muttered hopelessly.

'The water plants are what we've neglected,' Smooth Otter explained. 'Small quantities taken with our usual fare – fish – kept us healthy. We ate strands here and there almost without noticing. The plants have beneficial qualities. That's what our bodies are lacking now.'

Sleek Otter's mouth dropped open. 'You really think . . . I mean, it's that simple?'

'I'm sure of it,' Smooth Otter said with conviction.

'Then which plants – which plants must I gather?' the mother otter cried pitifully. 'My cubs are so weak; they can't walk as far as the holt entrance.'

'The plants in the stream,' Smooth Otter told her. 'The cressy plants that grow where the water runs swift and clear.'

'I know!' Sleek Otter whistled. 'I know the ones.' And she raced away as fast as she could go. She dived into the stream and paddled against the current. She knew exactly where she was heading. A bed of watercress where she had often fished for small fry was her destination. The plant was her cubs' only hope now. She swam intently. Other otters, who had listened to the big male's advice, were ahead of her. All the animals in the water converged on the thick tangle of cress. Without pausing for a word, Sleek Otter tore off mouthfuls of the deep green leaves with her sharp teeth. In a few moments she was swimming downstream again.

'I'm coming, my babies. I'm coming,' she murmured as her body rippled through the water, her fur glistening with silver where it had trapped pockets of air bubbles below the surface. She swooped up from the stream into her dry holt entrance and scattered the plant stems by the still bodies of her cubs. 'Eat this,' she commanded sharply. 'You must eat this. Please, please, eat!'

The young otters didn't stir. Their sufferings were over. Lean Vixen had wrought her revenge.

Sleek Otter was not the only one to mourn. Other youngsters succumbed as a result of eating the diseased voles. They hadn't the fortitude of the adult otters who had fallen sick. Those animals managed to recover after taking the measures advised by the big dog otter. They were suitably grateful and Smooth Otter began to be looked upon as a kind of leader. Now he believed more than ever in his own superiority.

After this scare, the otters tried to rely once more on their normal diet. The entire length of the stream and its surroundings were scoured for a viable food supply. There were small numbers of crayfish and mussels and some tench and roach, but the otters were only too aware that these prey could soon be exhausted. At the same time they knew they must steer clear of voles.

'We must return to the woods,' Smooth Otter said.

'The woods are dangerous,' another male argued. 'Do we want to poison ourselves again?'

Smooth Otter's whiskers twitched. 'We shall know better this time,' he said. 'We have no alternative but to hunt once more where the foxes, stoats and weasels catch their prey. We can learn from them. *They're* not sick. They must know which prey to avoid. So we watch them closely. We watch where they go, we watch what they catch and then –' he whistled assertively – 'we take it from them.'

'How do we take food from a fox?' the other male queried. 'An otter could never win a fight with a fox.'

'That's debatable,' was Smooth Otter's opinion, 'as it hasn't been proved one way or the other. And it probably never will be because, you see, we're not going to fight them.'

'Oh, so they'll just pass over their food to us when we ask for it?'

'Sarcasm is lost on me. Look – don't you remember how we showed the other predators how much quicker, how much more agile we are? Well, we can do so again, only this time we'll let them catch the prey first. When they've made a kill, we'll rush in and whisk it away before they know we're around.'

The smaller dog otter wasn't convinced. 'I'll come with you on your next hunting trip, then,' he remarked, 'and you can show me how it's done.'

Smooth Otter's confidence was unbounded. 'Nothing simpler,' he assured the other.

The Farthing Wood hunters had been lulled into a false sense of security. Lean Vixen and Sly Stoat had congratulated themselves on their clever plan and had reverted to being rivals. As the weather grew milder, prey was easier to find. The snow gradually melted and fox, stoat and weasel had their minds on other things. They followed the lean foxes' example and began to pair off.

Stout Fox's image of a suitable vixen was of a female with health and strength similar to his own. So when he found a stout-looking vixen tracking an old rabbit which he had singled out himself, he surrendered his interest in it and lay down to watch her tactics. The vixen was big for a female and appeared to have eaten well throughout the winter. This impressed Stout Fox at once. Here was a female who would have definite advantages as a mate. Under the eye of the old rabbit buck, she began to chase her tail. Stout Fox grinned as he saw the rabbit's puzzlement. The vixen twirled around as if she had nothing else on her mind except play. Every so often the rabbit nibbled at some herbage but it never lost sight of the vixen's antics. The animal was, if anything, rather curious about the female predator. It certainly didn't take fright. Stout Fox's tongue hung loose and he panted as he watched the vixen's dance take her closer and closer still to the rabbit without its least suspicion.

'You've had it, chum,' Stout Fox whispered prophetically.

The vixen began a final mad spin, ending with a beautifully timed pounce. The rabbit knew nothing about it. It was dead before it knew it was under threat.

Now Stout Fox rushed forward. 'Bravo,' he barked. 'A fine example of skill. Where have you been hiding yourself? I don't recall seeing you before.'

The vixen regarded him coolly. She guarded her kill in case Stout Fox's approach was some kind of ploy. Her face wore a very worldly expression as if she had seen everything before at least once. 'I don't hide,' she replied, 'but I cover a lot of ground.'

'You must do,' the fox acknowledged. 'Have you – er – ever encountered the otters?'

'Now and then. But not recently.'

Stout Fox was eyeing the rabbit.

'I suppose you're hoping to share my kill?' the vixen asked baldly.

'No. No. I merely watched you from interest and – and – admired what I saw.'

The stout vixen softened. 'Well, after all,' she resumed, 'there's more than enough for one. Do you have a permanent den? Mine's a long way off.'

'Yes.' Stout Fox was encouraged. 'My earth is in the side of a badger set. We get along.'

'Just as well,' the vixen commented. 'Show me the way then. We can share my catch in comfort.'

The fox wondered at her abrupt change of attitude but assumed she had seen something in him, at any rate, that she liked. He led her across a glade to a clearing in the Wood where the set was situated. The badgers were absent except for a young male who was rooting up worms near one of the entrances. Stout Fox and the badger recognized each other and paid no attention to one another's activities.

The stout vixen dropped the rabbit carcass on the sandy floor of the den. 'Hm. Comfortable-looking place,' she observed appreciatively, looking around and then sniffing the air.

'It suits me,' Stout Fox said.

'Might suit me too,' the vixen remarked.

Stout Fox wagged his tail. 'Sure to,' he replied. 'Look upon it as your own.'

Shortly after this episode the otters were once again seen in the Wood. Sly Stoat, who had recently acquired a mate also, was the first to fall victim to their new determination. Smooth Otter provided the demonstration the other otter required. He followed the stoat on its hunting run, allowed him to fell a shrew and then snatched it from his grip.

'Easy come, easy go,' he sneered at the stoat who was too stunned to react.

'You said to make use of the foxes; there was nothing about stoats,' the other otter said critically. 'I want to see how you tackle foxes.'

Smooth Otter glared. 'Stoat; fox; what does it matter?' he growled.

'There's a deal of difference between the two,' his companion insisted. 'Any of us can get the better of an animal the size of a stoat.'

Smooth Otter was stung into action. 'All right. You eat this shrew while I go for a bigger prize.' He dropped the stoat's kill. 'I can cope with foxes, don't you worry.'

'Mine, I think,' Sly Stoat muttered, snapping up the shrew and running for his den.

'Oh-ho, you're so slow you *need* lessons,' Smooth Otter derided the other male. 'Come on!'

There weren't any foxes in the neighbourhood just then. 'Look, forget what I said,' the slow male called to Smooth Otter after a while. 'I'm ravenous. Can't we just find our own food?'

The big leader otter ran on regardless. He was resolved, now his ability had been challenged, to demonstrate his prowess. Slow Otter, grumbling constantly, dropped farther and farther behind. Eventually he lost sight of the big male.

'Oh, to blazes with *him*,' he said to himself. 'I've had enough.' He stopped running. He had no idea where he was. He hadn't explored much of the woodland before. 'Now where on earth am I going to get something to eat?' As he looked around, wondering what to do next, he heard a tremendous commotion break out elsewhere in the Wood. Barking, shrieking, whistling, yapping – it sounded as though a really serious fight was taking place. Slow Otter this time was quick on his feet. With the inquisitiveness of all his kind he ran under the trees towards the din. Secretly he longed to find Smooth Otter in difficulties with a fiercer animal. He didn't take kindly to his boastful manner at all.

When he arrived on the scene the noise had ceased and there was a tug-of-war being enacted between Smooth Otter on the one hand and a very angry and determined Lean Vixen on the other. In the middle, with its legs in the jaws of the fox and its head clamped in the sharp teeth of the otter, was an unfortunate and very dead pheasant. Both animals had braced themselves, digging their feet into the damp soil and pulling hard. The vixen's greater strength began to tell. But with the arrival of Slow Otter her antagonist was spurred on to new efforts.

'Whatever is he doing?' Slow Otter muttered. 'This is a struggle he can't possibly win.'

Sure enough the carcass began to come apart. With a final wrench the vixen tore the body loose and Smooth Otter was left with only the pheasant's head in his mouth.

Lean Vixen dropped the bird. 'You stupid animal,' she snarled at Smooth Otter. 'Do you plan to wrest our food from our very jaws? What kind of madness will you get up to next? Be warned.' She turned to look at Slow Otter. 'You too,' she growled. 'Try those sort of tricks again and we foxes will drive you from the Wood!'

'You and who else?' muttered Smooth Otter. But it was his turn to feel humiliated and he turned to go.

Slow Otter followed. 'Just lead us back to the stream,' he urged his companion. 'There's nothing for us here.'

'There will be,' Smooth Otter vowed grimly. 'You don't think I give up that easily, do you?'

5. Omens

IN MARCH Farthing Wood was carpeted with banks of celandine and wood anemone. Primroses gleamed in the sunny glades and marsh plants sprouted along the stream's edges. Frogs, toads, newts and reptiles emerged from hibernation and, in the mammal world, hedgehogs woke and went about their business again.

One old creature, who had lived in the Wood for many seasons, was known as Sage Hedgehog because of his wisdom. During his long winter sleep he had experienced strange and striking dreams which he believed were some kind of premonition. He related them to those animals willing to listen.

'I saw a strange place with many animals. Animals such as us; such as those who live here. It was like Farthing Wood, yet it was not Farthing Wood. A beautiful antlered beast with the grace and carriage of a deer, but ghostly white, stood on its edge. On the one side was a poor broken piece of ground, barren of creatures and full of the noise and danger of humans and their works. On the other, rolling grassland and woodland. The white beast looked from one place, the one with nothing, to the place with the animals. Then it grew dark and the deer's white coat shimmered like a pale beacon in the gloom. All at once the beast disappeared and there was nothing but darkness. Over and over I have dreamed this dream. I believe there is a message in it; that it foretells the end of Farthing Wood.'

A group of hedgehogs who were listening stirred uneasily. They were puzzled and a little shaken. One of them said, 'Dreams are dreams. This could mean anything – or nothing.'

Sage Hedgehog looked at the animal steadily. 'There is a different air in Farthing Wood now,' he said. 'The Wood is threatened. I feel it in my bones. It's a new sensation. Before the winter I felt nothing and was content.'

'There's no evidence of a threat,' a young hedgehog said. 'Everything is just the same as when we began our sleep.'

Another hedgehog was more cautious. 'There have been other times when the sage one has spoken strange words. And I recollect when once he foretold a great storm and urged us to take shelter and we –'

'Yes, yes,' cut in another. 'We didn't take any notice of him and then there *was* a storm and some hedgehogs were drowned when the stream burst its banks. So what? Simply a coincidence, *I'd* say.'

'Well, I wouldn't,' the first hedgehog returned. 'He's something of a prophet in my view.'

'We shall see,' the second remarked. 'Do you detect any sign of change?'

There was no answer. Sage Hedgehog said, 'I sense disaster. I beg you, all of you, to be on your guard.' He went on his way, and left his fellows to make of his dreams what they would.

Other animals in Farthing Wood were to learn of the vision of the white deer. Some of them were impressed and felt concern, others were openly scornful. It didn't take much to unsettle the squirrels and rabbits who were always jumpy, whereas the weasels and stoats laughed at Sage Hedgehog behind his back.

'There's no fool like an old fool,' Quick Weasel chortled. 'That we should be taken in by his tales!'

Sly Stoat's wily mate commented, 'Time will tell. If his warnings prove correct, we shall remember them ruefully. In any case, what provision could any of us make?'

'He's ancient and his mind wanders and makes up pictures,' Quick Weasel chattered. 'There's always been a Farthing Wood and there always will be. We have the otters to thank for that,' she added explanatorily.

'Yes. That's their habitual refrain, isn't it?' Wily Stoat said. 'My mate and I are sick of hearing it. And what if one day there were no otters? Have you thought of that?'

'Of course,' Quick Weasel answered. 'But I don't worry myself. Otters don't suddenly disappear and they'll be around for as long as we are.'

The dispute over food and prey continued to occupy the foxes and otters. They had no time to take account of dreams or predictions. Smooth Otter hunted alone now. He had realized it was as well not to have witnesses to his success or failure. He steered clear of the mature, canny foxes, and concentrated on filching titbits from younger or weaker animals. His skill and dexterity usually paid dividends. The other otters were capitalizing on the spring gathering of frogs and newts in the water courses. For a while there was plenty for all, then abruptly the amphibians' brief mating season was over and the survivors dispersed throughout the Wood and sur-rounding grassland.

Smooth Otter ignored the frogs. He loved to pit his wits against rivals and whenever he bested them he never failed to crow about it.

A young badger, a male cub a few seasons old from the set where Stout Fox and his vixen lodged, fell victim to the dog otter's gibes. The badger had been about to eat a pigeon fledgling which had fallen from its nest. The otter had been shadowing the bulkier animal for a while without arousing suspicion, waiting to see what food the badger might turn up. The feeble fluttering of the injured fledgling had attracted the young badger's curiosity and, just as he was about to seize it, Smooth Otter dashed in, flicked the bird to one side with his paw and made off with it.

'Oh, how you woodland animals suffer when we otters are on your heels,' Smooth Otter boasted. 'You're a cumbersome lot, heavy-footed and ponderous.' He trotted to a distance of a few metres in case the badger was inclined to react.

Young Badger, however, was nonplussed. 'Why do you do this?' he asked with genuine bewilderment. 'Why do you make a game of everything? Eating isn't a game; it's how all of us keep the threads of life together.'

'Except when there's an otter on your tail!' the other animal laughed.

Young Badger looked sulky. 'It's no laughing matter,' he said. 'There's a time for play and – and –'

'And why didn't you join in our games, then, in the snow?' Smooth Otter interrupted.

'You wouldn't come, any of you. I came looking for high-spirited animals like you!'

'Oh yes, mock all you like,' Young Badger remarked, aware of the sarcasm. 'We can't all be athletes and swimmers, can we? We are as we're made. But you know, you're really rather silly. You seem set on annoying everyone. What for? It might rebound on you. My father, the kindly badger, always taught us youngsters we should get along with everyone as best we can, because in that way Farthing Wood thrives. But it seems *you're* set on disruption.'

'Disruption? No,' Smooth Otter chuckled. 'We just enjoy life whichever way we can. So catching prey can be as much fun for us as anything else. Too bad most of you are such a dull lot!' He bounded away, jigging this way and that around some chestnut saplings.

Young Badger watched and shook his head. 'I'm afraid otters and woodlanders simply don't blend,' he murmured.

*

When the glut of frogs was over for that spring, other otters had no alternative but to return to hunting small mammals. The badgers were not the only inhabitants of Farthing Wood who felt a crisis was looming. The squirrels and hedgehogs and many of the woodland birds, who were not among the hunted, watched the behaviour of the otters with alarm.

'Someone should t-try to c-calm them down,' Nervous Squirrel stammered. He sat on a high branch watching a pair of otters chasing Quick Weasel beneath the trees. 'They're so un*settling*.'

'Madness!' screeched Jay who couldn't keep still when there was any disturbance. He flew to another tree. 'Madness! The foxes are gathering, I've seen them. When they're not being robbed, they're being goaded and irritated.'

'Hunting calls for silence and perseverance,' an owl fluted from a hollow oak. 'I should know. There's just no peace and quiet any more.'

'W-why don't we t-tell them?' Nervous Squirrel chattered. 'Tell them to p-pipe down. And – and –'

'And respect the ways of others?' the owl suggested.

'Yes. Ex-exactly.'

'Some of us have tried, but the otters won't compromise. They're the jokers of the animal world. They have no seriousness.'

The foxes were indeed planning to take action. The youngsters had been tested to the limit and were looking for some support from their seniors. Groups of foxes began to debate their grievances and it was these gatherings that Jay had watched from the tree-tops. Lean Vixen backed up the young foxes.

'I warned the big otter about the consequences if he and his kind continued with their tricks,' she told a large group of all ages. 'My mate and I are ready to do whatever's necessary. It's time we struck a blow.'

Lean Fox hadn't been consulted about whether he was in agreement with this. He said nothing therefore, hoping the others wouldn't realize the vixen was dominant.

The young foxes related their experiences. Time and time again otters had interfered with their hunting techniques, sneaking prey from them and deriding them afterwards.

'It's intolerable,' said one. 'We can never hold our heads up again if we let them get away with it.'

'Otters or foxes,' Lean Vixen growled, 'one group has to come out on top.' She looked around the gathering and her eyes rested on Lean Fox. 'And it won't be the otters!'

'No. No, it won't be,' he concurred hastily. 'Tomorrow night we'll muster. All of us who care for our way of life – our fox ways – must take part. We'll chase those slippery pests from the Wood!'

Lean Vixen grinned a foxy grin. These were strong words; rousing words. The young foxes were satisfied. They ran off to carry the message to as many others of their kind in Farthing Wood as could be found.

The next evening the foxes rallied. With Stout Fox and Lean Vixen at their head, they trotted quietly through the depths of the Wood, intent on forestalling the otters close by the stream. Little light filtered through the budding branches but, at the edge of the woodland, the setting sun shone on the glistening water, turning it blood red. The foxes stood silently.

'It's an omen,' whispered a youngster. 'Blood will be shed.'

Stout Fox murmured grimly, 'Yes. I fear blood will flow if the otters persist in their ways.'

'You can count on it,' Lean Vixen snarled. 'Before the Wood is in leaf.'

6. One Trick Too Many

THERE was something about that evening that seemed to affect the entire population of Farthing Wood. The atmosphere was remarkably quiet. A spring breeze, a cool breeze, blew across the grassland. Nothing stirred. Not a single otter appeared. Were they suspicious? Lean Fox broke the silence.

'It doesn't look as if there's anything to chase after all,' he said.

'Give them time,' said Lean Vixen.

The sun sank below the horizon. Darkness cloaked the foxes and the stream ran black.

At last there was movement. Something approached, then turned and set off in another direction.

'Follow it,' Lean Vixen yapped. The foxes ran forward. The creature, which was indeed an otter, turned at the sound of running feet. Far from taking fright, it stood its ground. The foxes' rush slowed, then halted.

'Rather unfair odds, isn't it?' Sleek Otter asked, for it was she.

'Are you alone?' Stout Fox growled.

'You have eyes.'

'Then where are the others?' a young fox piped up.

'How should I know? In the Wood perhaps.'

'In the Wood?' Stout Fox barked. 'Nothing passed us as we came. How can that be?'

'Hardly likely they'd want to come face to face with a force of foxes,' Sleek Otter observed, 'if they *are* in the Wood.'

'What game is this?' Lean Vixen snarled.

'There is more than one way to enter a Wood,' was the reply and Sleek Otter tittered.

Lean Vixen was infuriated. Had the otters outmanoeuvred them again? While the foxes were standing idle, were they plundering the woodland in their absence?

'Back to the Wood!' she roared. 'They've gone behind our backs!'

The foxes, in one mass, turned and galloped towards the trees. Sleek Otter could hardly contain herself. She rolled over in her delight, whistling and giggling. Her cool-headedness had tricked the other animals into retreat. For she knew quite well not one otter, apart from herself, had yet left its holt.

Try as they might, and they searched high and low in twos and threes, the foxes couldn't find anything to chase. But their activity flushed some other creatures into the open. Amongst these were hedgehogs. The hedgehogs were very frightened, but soon realized the foxes were after different game. Sage Hedgehog unrolled himself and called to the others, 'We're safe for the moment. We're of no interest to them.'

Stout Fox paused to grunt, 'Not unless you can tell me if you've seen otters tonight.'

'No. None. Why do you seek them?'

'We're at loggerheads. Foxes and otters need to settle their differences and now there's only one way . . . '

'You wish to fight them?'

Stout Fox growled, 'If necessary. But certainly to frighten them.'

'Then we hedgehogs shall remain silent,' said the sage one bravely. 'Were we to see otters, we couldn't expose them to danger.'

'Very well. But we foxes will find them one way or another,' Stout Fox replied determinedly.

'We take no sides in your dispute,' the hedgehog continued. 'But we wish the otters no harm. Indeed their presence here must be preserved.'

'Not in Farthing Wood!' Stout Fox snapped. 'We have our own ideas about that!'

'Don't do anything we shall all regret,' Sage Hedgehog pleaded. 'If the otters go, I dread the consequences. You're more sensible than most. I appeal to you to avert a disaster.'

'Stuff and nonsense,' Stout Fox remarked dismissively. He knew all about Sage Hedgehog. 'You and your crackpot notions! Now listen to me. We foxes mean to keep the otters out of our territory. There's no two ways about that. And we'll use any means necessary.'

'No, no,' wailed Sage Hedgehog. 'We shall all be losers. Don't let the humans in!'

'Humans? They've been coming and going here ever since I can remember,' Stout Fox said and went on his way.

Sage Hedgehog's head sank on to his paws. More to himself than to any other creature he murmured sorrowfully, 'I fear the time will arrive when the humans come, but don't go.'

There was no discovery and no fighting that night. Sleek Otter made haste to give the news of the foxes' massing to her kind. The otters saw sense and decided to avoid confrontation. Smooth Otter, however, couldn't resist a retort.

'How we've impressed them all,' he quipped glibly. 'We've really ruffled their pride.'

'Well, we can't match them in strength,' Sleek Otter cautioned. 'You should have seen them. They looked an ugly lot.'

'Oh, they'll disband soon enough,' the big male assured her lightly. 'What can they do? They know they can't touch us.'

This was not at all how the foxes saw the situation.

They had reached the end of their tether. Stout Vixen, who had stayed behind in the den, greeted her mate's return with the words,

'I don't see any signs of a scrap. Your coat's as clean as a cat's.'

'There was no scrap,' Stout Fox admitted, 'because there were no otters.'

'I told you so,' said the vixen. 'You need to use more subtle methods with that bunch.'

'Perhaps we've frightened them off?'

'No. They'll slip back to the woodland unnoticed when things have quietened down.'

'What do you suggest then?'

'As the otters seem to bother you so much, there's only one course of action. Get rid of them altogether.'

'You mean – kill them?' Stout Fox muttered as though he hardly dared pronounce the words.

'Not all of them. When they see their lives are at stake they'll get the message soon enough and move out.'

Stout Fox baulked at the idea of wholesale slaughter. 'Let's hope they won't provoke us any further,' he said without much conviction.

*

Of course it wasn't in the nature of the otters to lie low. It was quite out of the question for them to be quiet or still for long. And, in any case, hunger asserted itself. They had to hunt whether they liked it or not. Some of them explored the grassland which surrounded the Wood and found a mouse or two. But this was a poor alternative to the rich fare offered by the Wood itself.

With the confidence born of their belief in their special status, the main bulk of the otters once more penetrated the woodland. They hunted singly and thoroughly. It was not long before they once more found themselves competing with the habitual woodland dwellers.

Smooth Otter, predictably, was the spark that lit the fatal fuse. His vanity made him incapable of heeding any warning signals. He forgot Sleek Otter's experience and set about stalking Lean Fox with the idea of relieving him of his catch. Lean Fox had set his sights on a young hare that was less watchful than it needed to be. Luckily for the young animal, it was able to make its escape. For, as Lean Fox closed, freezing every time the hare turned to look, Smooth Otter tried to circumvent his ploy. The otter's final dash, in front of the patient, painstaking fox, alarmed the hare who scooted away as swift as the wind.

Lean Fox, who had spent many long minutes carefully positioning himself, hurled himself on the culprit. He bowled the otter over and a vicious fight began. They were a match for each other.

The noise attracted onlookers. 'F-fox in a fight! Otter on the f-floor,' Nervous Squirrel skittered, leaping from branch to branch.

Sly Stoat hid behind a tree-trunk, peering round every now and then to watch the contest. As a predator, both animals were his rivals, but as a woodlander he was on the side of the fox. Smooth Otter gave a good account of himself. He was strong and supple and quick-footed. Lean Fox found it impossible to get a grip on him. Equally, the otter's smaller stature didn't allow him to gain advantage.

'It's l-level pegging,' Nervous Squirrel squeaked to anyone who cared to listen.

'Keep quiet,' said Owl. 'Let them sort it out.'

Smooth Otter, jigging to right and left, and nipping the fox's tail or leg whenever he got the chance, resorted to taunts. 'Catch me if you can, Fox. Whoops! Missed me! Where am I now? No, not there. Here! Clumsy fox!'

The bigger animal was panting heavily and beginning to look confused. Then Lean Vixen rushed up and the scales were tilted. The two foxes together were too much for the athletic otter. If he avoided one's attack, he stepped right into the other's. He received a succession of deep bites and suddenly wilted. The Wood was quiet. The onlookers held their breath, expecting a kill. The foxes lunged on both sides. Smooth Otter rolled over, bleeding from a dozen gashes.

'He's done for,' Lean Vixen panted. 'Leave him.'

Lean Fox stepped back and looked at the stricken animal. His sides heaved from his exertions.

'D-death, death of an otter!' shrilled Nervous Squirrel.

The cry was taken up by a host of other small animals and the news spread through the Wood like wildfire. Other creatures came running; badgers, weasels, rabbits, hedgehogs. Elsewhere the foxes heard the cry and responded. Their blood was up. Four other otters were cornered in the Wood and pulled down by their long-suffering adversaries. Another was caught and savaged as she raced for safety to the stream. Stout Fox took no part in the killing. He restricted himself to running along the Wood's perimeter and driving others on who were trying to escape. The otters were vanquished. Those who survived abandoned their holts and ran for their lives, believing the foxes would massacre them all if they stayed.

By dawn not a single otter was left in Farthing Wood.

The foxes came together in the centre of the Wood, grimly satisfied with their work. They were not yet aware that the surviving otters had disappeared for good and indeed were at that moment still running across country under cover of darkness.

'It had to be done,' Lean Vixen spoke for all of her kind. She panted deeply. Many of the foxes still simmered from the heat of battle. They had not escaped unscathed. The otters' sharp teeth and claws had left their mark. Blood lust still glinted in some eyes. The foxes were ready for more killing if any creature dared to cross them. For the moment none did and, gradually, their fighting ardour cooled.

'The Wood's ours again,' Stout Fox said. 'But surely we could have achieved that without such extreme savagery?'

The animals returned to their own territories, certain that no otter would ever presume to set foot in them again. They couldn't have known that their action would mean that, in the long run, their lives would change for ever.

7. Aftermath

THE STOATS and weasels were astir soon after the foxes' attack. Sly Stoat found Smooth Otter's carcass and sniffed at it inquisitively.

'Your arrogance put paid to you,' he murmured to the dead animal. 'You wouldn't be told. What's your so-called superiority worth now?' He laughed a stoat laugh. 'A feast for the worms, that's all.' He trotted away, his movements brisker than for a long while.

Quick Weasel had attracted a mate and was oblivious of anything that happened around her. The male weasel was dark and quicker even than she: lightning-fast. He circled her and chased her and they ran through the flower carpet, tumbling and sparring like two kittens. In places the ground was tainted with blood. Where the weasels rolled it flecked their glossy coats with dark spots. They groomed themselves and continued their courtship, forgetful and careless of others' dramas. Life and its continuation was all that mattered to them.

In the badgers' ancient set Kindly Badger spoke to his son. 'The foxes reacted as I feared,' he said. 'The otters were too clever for them and they resented it.' He pressed down some fresh bedding and lay on it. 'We had no part in it and yet . . . '

'Yet what, Father?'

'And yet we *are* part of it,' Kindly Badger seemed to contradict himself. 'We're part of Farthing Wood, just as they are. We can't remain unaffected.'

'Didn't you always believe animals can get along together if they . . . if they . . . ' Young Badger groped for the words.

'If they respect each other? Yes,' Kindly Badger mumbled. He was feeling drowsy. 'But it doesn't always work out that way. You can't respect a creature who is' – he yawned widely – 'taking the food from your mouth.'

Farthing Wood warmed itself in the spring sunshine. The night creatures had gone to their rest. Nervous Squirrel called to his family, 'S-strangers in the Wood! Take care!' as he always did when humans approached. The squirrels leapt through the tree-tops, pausing to squint down at the two people who were bending over the remains of Smooth Otter.

'Four,' one man said to his companion. 'What's been happening here?' His distress was unmistakable. The other human shook her head and the two trudged on, systematically searching the Wood bottom.

'Slaughter!' Jay screeched at them but the startled bird was ignored.

By the stream-side the naturalists loitered, vainly waiting for a reassuring appearance of a bobbing head and whiskers in the water or a frisky somersault amongst the reeds. They stared long and hard, never talking and barely shifting their limbs. There was no comfort here. The stream was barren except for a skulking moorhen or two. They walked along its banks, then the woman grabbed the man's arm and pointed at the muddy ground. Fresh tracks, otter tracks, made by several animals led away from the stream and away from Farthing Wood itself. They followed them where they could, but the tracks were soon lost amongst rank grass. Even so the naturalists were left in no doubt that some serious misfortune had overtaken the protected animals. It was now their prime objective to discover their fate.

*

Seven animals, including Sleek Otter, had fled the foxes' wrath. At first they had run in a blind panic. Then, with distance behind them, they eased up and listened for sounds of pursuit.

'It's quiet,' Sleek Otter whispered.

'Shall we go back?' another female suggested, gazing forlornly across the grassland.

'To certain death,' Slow Otter told her bluntly. 'The big dog otter, the smooth one, brought havoc among us. He courted danger and thought himself invincible. But he put the foxes in a frenzy.'

'Where shall we go then?'

'Why ask me? My world, like yours, was small. I know nothing else.'

'We should head for a waterway,' said Sleek Otter. 'Our stream wasn't isolated. It must empty into another.'

'But where?'

'I don't know.'

'We should search for other otters,' another animal urged.

'There *are* no other otters,' she was told. 'We're the last for miles and miles. We grew up knowing that. How can you have forgotten?'

'I hadn't forgotten. But – but – what else can we do?'

'Go on until we find somewhere bearable,' said Sleek Otter, 'or . . . or . . . die in the attempt.'

They ran on, close-knit, not daring to stray. The grassland gave way to empty fields, then roads, the smell of smoke, moving lights and frightening sounds.

'We're lost,' shrilled a youngster.

'Of course we're lost,' said Slow Otter. 'From now on, we'll always be lost.'

It became apparent eventually to the inhabitants of Farthing Wood that the otters had vanished. There were few regrets but some misgivings.

'What will it mean?' Wily Stoat asked her mate.

'Only that there's more food for everyone,' Sly Stoat answered cynically.

'But they were always full of such tales.'

'Tales of their own importance, yes. Well, we can get along without them. All in all they were a tiresome bunch.'

The wise hedgehog was troubled by more dreams. Once again the vision of the white deer disturbed his daytime sleep, now with more urgency. The deer had advanced and seemed larger and more distinct. Sage Hedgehog knew then that it fell to him to impress on the other animals that some menace hovered over Farthing Wood; that in some way they must make changes to avert an awful fate.

The other hedgehogs heard him out. 'There are no changes we can make that would make a jot of difference to Farthing Wood one way or the other,' commented one. 'We cause no disturbance. We take what we need and don't interfere with the lives of other creatures.'

Sage Hedgehog said, 'None of us can escape the doom that threatens us, from the smallest to the largest. Unless . . . '

'Unless what?' an elderly hedgehog asked. 'Unless we sprout wings and fly away? Your riddles are of little help.'

'Unless,' Sage Hedgehog murmured, 'we somehow pull together to – to –' he screwed up his eyes as he struggled to find words to interpret what seemed to him a message from some mystical source – 'to save ourselves,' he finished in a burst with a long sigh of relief.

'It's the larger animals who can affect what changes take place here, and only they,' another hedgehog said. 'The foxes are the most powerful animals as they've already demonstrated. Take your tale to them. I doubt if they'll listen, but if *they* don't, your breath is wasted on any other creature.'

'I shall speak to the foxes,' Sage Hedgehog confirmed. 'I shall speak to everyone.'

*

As before, few of the Wood's inhabitants were inclined to listen. Sage Hedgehog persisted. It was his role to warn others and not to be defeated by apathy or scorn.

'You were wrong to make war with the otters,' he told the foxes. 'You will rue the day you drove them out.'

'On the contrary,' Lean Vixen corrected him. 'It's the best thing we ever did. Look how we've benefited.' She and her mate had filled out considerably, and their coats had a healthy sheen. 'We've taken on a new lease of life.'

'A lease that will end abruptly in disease and panic,' Sage Hedgehog predicted.

'You dotty old ball of spikes,' Lean Vixen scoffed, half angrily and half in amusement. 'You come to us with this nonsense and expect us to take you seriously?'

'A threat to the Wood is surely serious?' Lean Fox cautioned.

'What threat? There's no evidence –'

'There have been more humans in the Wood of late,' Lean Fox interrupted.

'Oh, we pay them too much attention,' the vixen dismissed his remark. 'We always have. But why? They never do anything. They walk, they look . . . what sort of threat is that?'

'Human interest can always be a threat,' Lean Fox muttered sullenly. 'I'd prefer to be ignored.'

Sage Hedgehog said, 'If the human eye is on us, we'd do well to look out for each other.'

Meanwhile the otters, torn between their fear of the unknown and their horror of returning to their homes, made makeshift dens under a hedgerow and ate vegetation, snails and slugs to avoid starvation.

Sleek Otter determined to look for water. She knew that without it their lives were worth nothing.

8. The Otters' Plight

AT SUNSET one dry evening, four days after their flight, Sleek Otter set out. She slipped away while the others made their weary and fruitless search for nourishment. She had eaten almost nothing since abandoning her holt. She knew that the best way to find food was to find water. The memory of her cubs' deaths after eating unsuitable prey remained with her.

The air was balmy and still. She loped across a field. On the far side a road loomed – for the moment quiet. Sleek Otter sprinted across without pausing. Her heart beat fast. She sniffed the aroma of human food and human bodies hanging thickly in a cottage garden. Her nostrils twitched. Her whiskers brushed a wall as she ran along its length, then she slipped through a gate into the garden and trotted noiselessly to a garden pond. Her eyes widened. The scent of water lured her like a magnet. Noises from the house – a televised voice, the laughter of a viewer – made her hesitate. Then silence resumed.

Sleek Otter dived joyfully into the pond. It was tiny and clogged with weed, but the feel of water over her back and head was exhilarating. A terrified frog leapt for safety on to a water-plant. In a flash Sleek Otter seized it and her teeth crunched on her first real prey for days. The frog tasted delicious. The otter's eyes closed in sheer enjoyment, but her hunger was merely irritated by this mouthful and seemed greater than ever.

And then she found them. Nestling nervously amongst the weed and trying to stay hidden: goldfish. Sleek Otter whistled with excitement. One, two, three fish about the size of carrots and with no escape route.

'There's only one place you can go,' Sleek Otter told the luckless goldfish as she savoured the moment. 'And that's' – crunch – 'in here!' She gulped them down and then searched the entire pond for anything else that was edible. There was nothing more.

Reluctantly she pulled herself out and shook a fountain of spray from her coat. She thought of the six other otters scratching for morsels along the hedge bottom. The goldfish had put new heart into her. Perhaps there were more fish to be found nearby?

Slow Otter had hardly bothered to look for food at all. He was the most pessimistic of the seven and already believed that death for all of them could only be a matter of days away.

He watched the only other male grimly chewing an earthworm with an expression of distaste on his face.

'You can't put off the inevitable,' he told him. 'Bird food won't keep us alive.'

The other male limped from a wound sustained in a fight with a young fox. 'Maybe,' he grunted. 'But we can't simply curl up and die.'

'Might as well,' was Slow Otter's opinion. 'Oh,' he moaned, 'my stomach's as hollow as a rotten log.'

The four bitch otters had scattered on their own quests. One still had thoughts of returning some day to her deserted holt by Farthing stream. 'I could slip in unnoticed,' she told herself. 'A single otter doesn't make much of a splash. No one would suspect.' Then she thought about what an endlessly solitary existence would be like and shuddered. 'No. That's not sensible,' she said mournfully. 'I can't go alone. I must have a companion.' She turned to glance back at the two males. There was not much encouragement to be had there. She sighed forlornly and turned again to her foraging.

Sleek Otter left the cottage garden and found herself in a wide muddy expanse planted with vegetables. She threaded her way through these, turning every so often to make sure she wasn't observed. Another field stretched ahead. There was no sign or smell of water in that direction. She paused, reminding herself of the little pond and its situation near a human dwelling. Perhaps that was the key to other stocks of fish. Sleek Otter decided to seek out similar habitations.

There was a collection of buildings comprising a bungalow and various outhouses within easy distance of the vegetable field. Sleek Otter ran determinedly towards it. Desperation made her bold. She pattered cautiously into a yard. Everything was quiet enough. In the darkness the unmistakable sound of swishing water reached her ears. She trotted swiftly forward to investigate. She found six huge, round metal-sided vats spaced around the yard. These were sunk deep into concrete so that the tops were about a metre above ground level. Hosepipes ran to and from each, draining and replenishing water in a continual cycle. Every so often a splash or a plunge could be heard in one of the tanks. There were things moving in them – living things. Sleek Otter was filled with excitement. She ran to the nearest container and leapt up, balancing herself on the tank's rim.

'Fish!' she whistled. 'Hordes of them!' She watched the writhings and weavings of hundreds of plump silver trout. There were so many fish, there scarcely seemed to be a space unfilled. The water was literally alive with them. They were feeding from the remains of a scattering of pellets thrown in earlier by human hand. Sleek Otter's hungry eyes almost popped out of her head. Here at last was real prey – unlimited prey – for the taking. She watched the trout's darting movements as though mesmerized. She knew she must inform the other otters about this miraculous find. First, however, she meant to taste the trout for herself.

She contemplated diving headfirst into the vat, but resisted the temptation. She hooked a good-sized fish from the water which fell with a splat on to the ground where it wriggled furiously. Sleek Otter bounded after it, trapping it with her front paws and killing it with one deep bite to the neck. The flesh was pink and delicious. She ate with the heightened relish of an animal starved of its natural prey for too long.

'This place will be the saving of us,' she told herself afterwards. 'I must get back to the others.'

Cautious as ever, Sleek Otter retraced her journey. Luckily the road was once more deserted and she crossed it again without any alarm. She was soon reunited with the other six fugitives. They showed no particular interest at first in her return. All of them were thoroughly dispirited.

'Cheer up,' Sleek Otter rallied them. 'I've the best news possible. There's a mass of fish just waiting to be eaten.'

'Things are bad enough without your jokes,' Slow Otter grumbled. 'Of course there are fish, plenty of them. We know that. But exactly where they are is what we *don't* know.'

'You don't understand,' Sleek Otter chattered. 'I've found them! Only a short journey from here. There's more than enough for all of us. All we have to do is to take care. Believe me, it couldn't be simpler. We must move from here and find convenient dens nearer the place with the fish where we can hide during daylight. Now, who's ready to join me?'

The others gaped at her, still not entirely convinced by her tale. No one spoke.

'Well, what's the matter with you all?' Sleek Otter cried in exasperation. 'Aren't you hungry?'

'I'll come with you,' the lame otter said, 'if you promise to go slowly.'

'Can't be too slow,' she replied. 'We must get under cover before dawn.'

'I'll do my best,' he said.

The bitch otters began to look excited. 'And are there really fish . . . like we used to eat in the stream?' one asked longingly.

'Better. Bigger,' Sleek Otter told her triumphantly.

'Have you found a river?' another one breathed, picturing an idyllic watercourse.

'Er – no. Not exactly,' Sleek Otter replied hesitantly, then added, 'but there is water, naturally. And plenty of it.'

The six looked less eager. 'Is it a stream then?' Slow Otter queried.

'No. Not a stream.'

'A pond?' Lame Otter suggested. 'Like in Farthing Wood?'

'A sort of pond, I suppose,' Sleek Otter answered vaguely. 'But stop your questions, do! Come and see for yourselves!'

'Do we have any choice?' Slow Otter muttered. 'If we stay here, we'll certainly perish.'

Lame Otter was weak; weaker than the rest. Like most of the others, he hadn't eaten properly for several days. He took his time going across the first field. One of the bitch otters kept pace with him sympathetically. Sleek Otter reached the road together with the three other females. Slow Otter was some distance behind them and the other two brought up the rear.

'Make haste,' Sleek Otter shrilled to the stragglers. Although she was unfamiliar with roads and traffic, she sensed this strip of tarmac posed a threat. It smelt of danger, humans and sour fumes. The bitch otters loped across. Slow Otter reached the verge. They all heard a distant sound of an engine. Something approached. Frightened, Slow Otter accelerated and joined the leaders. The noise increased. Lame Otter and his companion weren't sure whether to go on or turn back.

'Quickly,' urged the safe animals. They knew they must get out of sight.

Lame Otter hesitated, then continued. A motorbike's headlamp gleamed menacingly, its beam brightening by the second as the machine roared nearer. Lame Otter, terrified, attempted a spurt. In the middle of the road he was caught in the gleam of the powerful lamp. The motor-cyclist braked. Lame Otter limped across, but his female companion stupidly turned to run back. She was too late and the sound of screeching brakes was followed by a dull thud. The rider almost toppled and only brought his machine under control with difficulty. The female straggler was killed instantly. The rest of the otters, panic-stricken, dashed on, not even giving a backward glance to their lost companion. The motor-cyclist bent glumly over the dead animal. He was shaken by the accident. He had never seen otters in that locality before and wondered at the cause of their sudden appearance.

9. The Trout Farm

THE SIX surviving otters scattered, unaware that their plight had become the focus of attention. Sleek Otter found that only two females remained with her. The other had dashed blindly to the nearest hiding-place. After a while the lone female found her way back to her friends. The two males lay low in a ditch. Gradually their fright subsided.

'Now what?' Slow Otter grunted.

'Try to find the fish, of course,' Lame Otter answered sharply.

'Only the sleek one knows where they are, and we've lost her,' grumbled the pessimistic dog otter.

'Then we must track her. It's our only hope.'

There was no time to be lost and, despite his painful limp, Lame Otter was the more resolute of the two. He picked up the bitches' scent and began to call. After a while the two males heard a response.

'They're not far away,' the lame animal remarked confidently. 'We may yet taste fish before the night's out.'

The four females arrived in the yard of the trout farm. Sleek Otter showed the three newcomers how she had found the water. 'Listen! It's unmistakable, isn't it? And you can hear those fat fish moving around. We'll have many a feast to make up for our fast!'

The ravenous females gulped in anticipation. 'Show us how you catch them,' one begged.

Sleek Otter, who was feeling noticeably stronger since her evening haul of goldfish and trout, ran towards the first tank and leapt gracefully to the top. Her balance was perfect. Moments later four large fish had been hooked from the water. The watching females fell upon these voraciously. Sleek Otter rejoined them, contenting herself with a few mouthfuls.

The trout had scarcely been swallowed when the two male otters called from nearby. They were answered at once.

'I can smell that you've eaten,' Slow Otter announced as he came into the yard. He and Lame Otter were drooling. They noticed scraps of fish bone and skin on the ground and snatched them up hastily as though afraid the females might take them.

'Wouldn't you prefer whole prey?' Sleek Otter asked them archly. She was in her element, aware of her supremacy in the group.

'What a stupid question!' Slow Otter rasped. 'Where are the fish? Point me in the direction.'

By way of an answer Sleek Otter repeated her performance. The glistening trout smacked on to the ground where their futile wriggles were swiftly halted. The two males gulped them down – heads, tails and bones. Nothing was left.

'I can get you as many as you like,' Sleek Otter boasted gleefully.

'Huh! The great provider,' Slow Otter mumbled ungraciously with his mouth full. 'Don't worry. What you can do, we can do too.'

'Speak for yourself,' Lame Otter said to him. 'There's no way in which *I* could get to the fish.'

'I'll look after you,' Sleek Otter beamed. She wanted to be appreciated by the males. 'We can make a new start here, all of us. Our old life's finished, but there's no reason why our new life can't be better.'

'If only we'd had such fish in Farthing Wood stream,' sighed the female who still hankered after her old home. 'None of the otters would have lost their lives and all those awful events wouldn't have happened.' She brushed some fragments of food from her whiskers which were exceptionally long.

The others were silent as they digested her words. Each one thought about the fateful lack of food which had caused them to be driven out into a perilous and unknown world. Finally Slow Otter said, 'The sky is paling. We should find shelter quickly: the humans will be astir.'

The six looked around for reliable cover. Sleek Otter had noticed a lake close to the trout farm which was fringed with reeds and other growth. It seemed the obvious place to hide in during the coming day. There would be time later to develop more permanent dens. She led them to it and the otters tunnelled into the vegetation, weary but at least no longer hungry. For a while they talked about the extraordinary bounty of fish. Although they couldn't, of course, understand the concept of a trout farm, they all knew the fish were where they were because of human intent. They knew that the fish must be of value to humans, which meant they – the otters – must exercise extreme care. It was obvious to them that their interference in the humans' plans must not be discovered, otherwise they would be in real danger.

'We need to make sure there's not a trace of our coming,' Sleek Otter summarized. 'It would perhaps be wise to bring the fish to eat here, or wherever we settle eventually.'

'Yes, that's sensible,' Lame Otter agreed. 'We don't want to attract the slightest attention to ourselves.'

Ironically that is exactly what the otters had done. News of the sighting in an area well away from their Farthing Wood habitat reached the local wildlife groups. These were puzzled and concerned. Why had the animals left their usual territory so suddenly? What had caused them to stray into an area of human population? An investigation into this mystery became vital. While the otters were using every ounce of caution, interested parties were combing the area around Farthing Wood for a clue to their present location. It was now generally accepted that there had been some kind of assault upon them by other animals – the dead otters were proof of that – and that, to escape further slaughter, the remaining otters had fled. It was the business of the conservation groups to secure these animals again, return them to their home territory, and ensure that they were properly protected there.

The inhabitants of Farthing Wood naturally knew none of this. None of them realized the chain of events that had been set in motion by the foxes' attack. Only Sage Hedgehog sensed impending disaster. His words, in the main, fell on deaf ears. Spring broods of young voles, shrews and fieldmice increased the little creatures' numbers dramatically. From owls to weasels, none of the predators went short of food. Rabbits, too, were breeding prolifically, so that the foxes' diet was a particularly good one.

Stout Fox and his vixen were the most skilled rabbit hunters, the vixen especially. 'You have a talent all your own,' Stout Fox told her after he had watched her admiringly for the umpteenth time. 'I can't think why you lay low while the otters made such nuisances of themselves. You could have shown them a thing or two.'

'I didn't lie low,' she corrected him. 'I simply kept apart. All that fuss! You were overawed, all of you, by their antics. Silly beasts, they only deserved to be ignored.'

They trotted home companionably in the moonlight. Ahead of them, they saw Lean Vixen flit like a shadow between two tall trees. The fox pairs didn't encounter one another very often. They preferred not to mingle, now that the fighting was done. But this time Lean Vixen caught the scent of the other two and turned towards them.

'You are well?' Stout Fox asked her, noticing the improvement in her appearance.

'Yes. And you?' Lean Vixen returned, assessing the big male's fitness.

'Well too,' came the reply. 'But some animals seem sickly.'

The lean vixen's ears pricked up. She remembered the trail of disease she had strewn in the path of the otters. 'What's the reason?' she asked.

'Who knows? It could be anything. But sometimes I have a strange feeling that the Wood itself is sickly.'

Lean Vixen's eyes narrowed. 'Has that old windbag of a hedgehog got to you?'

'Nothing to do with him,' Stout Fox declared. 'There *was* disease in the Wood, though, and it may still be around.'

*

For some days the supply of trout sustained all six otters without interruption. Sleek Otter brought food for the lame male as she had promised. Slow Otter and the other three females were able to catch their own. They soon became proficient at jumping to the edge of the tanks, balancing, and whipping out with their paws as much fish as they needed. Slow Otter became increasingly irritated by the way the lame male was pampered. The six otters were living in unnaturally close proximity to each other and there were bound to be ructions sooner or later.

'Why can't he fetch his own food?' he complained, casting a withering glance at Lame Otter who was accepting the latest catch as though it were his right.

'You know why,' Sleek Otter answered quietly. She was developing a sort of motherly fondness for the lame male.

'We others put ourselves at risk every time we go to the Metal Ponds,' Slow Otter muttered grudgingly. The 'Metal Ponds' was their name for the tanks. 'It's all very well lying around waiting to be fed like some drone.'

'I don't lie around,' Lame Otter defended himself. 'I roam here and there. I try to do for myself what I can, but I can't catch enough in the open water to feed myself properly. You've swum in it. You know there's almost nothing to catch.'

'Oh yes,' Slow Otter sneered, 'but I'm sure you prefer being dependent. It's such an easy life.'

'Easy life? How would you like to have this injury? I'm stuck with it whether I like it or not. It'll never heal.'

Slow Otter's grumbling subsided, only to return on another occasion. There was no doubt that all the females showed a preference for Lame Otter, partly because of his condition with which they sympathized, but also because he had a nicer nature. Slow Otter was jealous. One night his resentment boiled over.

It was the fifth night of the raids on the trout stocks. He and the four bitch otters pattered quietly across the yard; as usual Sleek Otter was first on to the tank. She caught her fish and two of the other females followed. Then Slow Otter and the last female went together. Slow Otter was eager, but the female was faster than he was. She sprang up to the rim, leaving the male on the ground seething with impatience. He trotted up and down, unable to keep still, glaring up balefully every so often at the female who seemed to be taking longer than normal.

'What's keeping you?' he growled. 'I'm famished.'

The bitch otter said, 'I'll be finished in a moment. I just want to find a bigger fish for the lame one. I don't think he's getting enough to eat.'

Slow Otter exploded. '*What?*' he screeched. This was too much. While the other females hastily left the yard with their catches, he scrambled up the tank, determined not to wait any longer. The female at the top overbalanced and fell with a deep splash into the water. The trout thrashed about in terror, making the contents of the tank resemble a whirlpool. Slow Otter found it almost impossible to target a particular fish in this melee. He raked the surface blindly with his claws and managed to seize one moderately sized trout. He had to be content with this.

Meanwhile the female otter had broken surface and was struggling to free herself. The water level was well below the rim of the vat and she couldn't find the purchase to drag herself out. Moreover the swirling water continually dragged her back so that she had to battle to overcome its force as well. She was in very real danger.

'Help! Help me!' she pleaded in a scared voice.

'Serves you right,' Slow Otter grunted. 'You'll have plenty of opportunity to find the biggest fish now.' And he jumped to the ground feeling rather pleased with his retort. He picked up his one fish and left the yard without experiencing a trace of guilt.

However, he ate alone and avoided his companions afterwards by swimming out to the middle of the lake. There was an islet there where a few ducks were sleeping. The birds awoke and quacked nervously, waddling to the water's edge and paddling away. Later in the night Sleek Otter became aware of the absence of the unfortunate female.

'Where is your sister?' she asked one of her companions. 'You usually stay close together.'

'I don't know. I fear something bad has happened.' She called her sister from the safety of the reeds.

'Perhaps we should go and look for her?' suggested the long-whiskered female.

'I'll go,' Lame Otter volunteered. 'Let me do something for you for a change.'

'No,' the missing bitch's sister replied. 'I'll go. She and I are from the same litter. I can't rest unless I find her. The slow one was with her. He hasn't returned either.'

'He's on the island,' Lame Otter said. 'I saw him swimming.'

'Alone?'

'Yes.'

'Then I'm more afraid than ever.' The female slipped through the reeds.

'Be careful of the humans. They awake as the light returns,' Lame Otter cautioned her, as they watched her hurry away.

10. Sickness

LATER that day the drowned otter was discovered in the tank. While searching for her, her unfortunate sister had been caught by the farm dog and killed before its owner could intervene. The man at the trout farm knew a bit about wildlife and was aware that no otters had lived in his neck of the woods in living memory. Once again the local conservation bodies were alerted. A search of the area immediately around the trout farm was hastily scheduled. The otters were losing their lives at an alarming rate. If there were any still alive, it was crucial to save them before any further accidents should occur. As for the trout, they had their tanks fitted with wire netting to protect them during the night . . .

Sleek Otter and her two companions had waited in vain for the reappearance of the missing females. They had heard the dog's barks while they cowered amongst the reeds. They had not run, for where else could they go? But as daylight broadened, their fears grew. Slow Otter remained at a distance, sensing that he had been the cause of some misfortune.

'The slow one hasn't shown himself,' Lame Otter said unnecessarily as the three huddled in the vegetation. 'Why is he keeping away?'

They all suspected he was avoiding them deliberately. 'We shall see him tonight when he's hungry,' said Long-Whiskers. 'Then he'll have some explanation.'

The daylight hours crawled by. The otters dreaded to hear the sounds of the dog. At last dusk arrived again and they began to breathe a little more easily. But they didn't move until well into the night hours.

Sleek Otter and Long-Whiskers left the lame male behind and timidly made their way, a few paces at a time, to the yard. They found that the first tank – where the female had been drowned – had been emptied and cleaned. This in itself was a shock. They hesitated. There was no sign of Slow Otter.

'What shall we do now?' Long-Whiskers squeaked.

'There are other fish here,' Sleek Otter replied, trying to sound more confident than she actually was.

When they had checked the remaining tanks only to find the trout safely wired off, they knew there was now no choice for them but to move. 'The humans must have taken our two friends,' Sleek Otter remarked sadly.

This was a heavy blow. They were such a little band of animals that each new loss seemed to presage their own extinction. 'I think we should go home,' Long-Whiskers murmured. 'We don't seem able to survive out here.'

'Neither in Farthing Wood,' Sleek Otter whispered. She turned to her companion. 'We'll see what the lame one thinks,' she said. She didn't mention Slow Otter, although they both wondered where he was.

Lame Otter welcomed them back, but he could see at once that something was wrong.

'What did you find?' he asked.

Sleek Otter described what they had seen.

'No food then?'

'No. But I'm not hungry anyway.'

'Nor I,' Long-Whiskers agreed. 'You see, there are more important things on our minds now than filling our stomachs.'

'She thinks we should go home,' Sleek Otter explained.

'But we don't have a home, do we?' Lame Otter pointed out. 'In Farthing Wood we are at the mercy of the foxes. Unless we prefer to starve to death.'

'I share your sentiments,' Sleek Otter agreed. She looked at Long-Whiskers. 'You must return if you wish,' she told her. 'But you'll be on your own.'

Long-Whiskers sighed. 'Then I'll stay with you,' she answered fatalistically.

'Good. And now we must leave here,' said Sleek Otter. 'It seems our fate forbids us to settle anywhere permanently.'

'Do we wait for the other male?' Lame Otter asked half-heartedly.

'I think the slow one prefers his own company,' was Sleek Otter's opinion.

No more was said on the subject. The three animals set off. Lame Otter was glad. He hoped not to encounter Slow Otter again.

*

The next day the search for the otters around the trout farm began. By then the three refugees had travelled a considerable distance and were hiding in a hollow log on a railway embankment. They had eaten nothing on the way.

Slow Otter had trailed them, always keeping sufficiently far behind so that his presence wasn't noticed. He followed the three instinctively, unwilling to make one of their party, yet rejecting the alternative of complete isolation.

Meanwhile in Farthing Wood more of the animals had sickened. It was the smaller hunters – the stoats and weasels – who were suffering. The pick of prey always went to the foxes, particularly now there were no otters to compete with them. There was no shortage of food for the smaller predators, but they weren't able to be selective. Some of the voles from the colony affected by disease had survived and managed to breed. They and their offspring were still carriers of a parasite, which meant that those who ate them felt the consequences. And these voles had spread throughout the Wood. Their appearance was different. They looked less plump, less bright-eyed, and were not so nimble in their movements. These signs were evident, yet not always recognized by hungry weasels or stoats.

Quick Weasel was the most noticeable casualty. Her usual darting runs and mercurial movements had deserted her. She appeared strangely lethargic. Her mate, by comparison, seemed lightning-fast.

'Qu-quick Weasel's become Slow W-Weasel,' cried Nervous Squirrel from a tree-stump. 'Her mate c-catches her food for her.'

Lightning Weasel overheard. 'As long as I don't catch anything *from* her,' he muttered through gritted teeth.

Sly Stoat saw his own mate sicken. He knew all about unsavoury voles, since he had been party to the poisoning of the otter cubs. He felt this was a kind of retribution.

'I told you to steer clear of voles,' he reminded Wily Stoat sharply. 'Couldn't you have listened?'

'I did listen,' she replied faintly as she lay groaning in their den. 'But when you make a quick kill you don't always have time – oh! oh! – to see what you've caught before you – oh! – eat it.'

'Well, eat these mice I've brought you. Perhaps you'll feel better.'

'I-I couldn't. I couldn't eat at all. Oh, I feel so, so poorly. I don't think I'll ever eat again.'

'Don't say that,' Sly Stoat beseeched her. 'That sounds like –'

'I know,' she cut in before he could spell it out. 'I know what it sounds like. I really think . . . I've done for myself.'

'It's the legacy of the otters,' Sly Stoat whispered to himself. 'It's revenge for what we did to them. I must see the old hedgehog. Perhaps he has some advice.'

Sage Hedgehog could often be found near Farthing Pond. There were sedges there whose leaves attracted snails and slugs, his favourite food. Sly Stoat heard the hedgehog smacking his lips over a glutinous morsel before he actually spied him. Sage Hedgehog saw him first.

'Troubled times,' he said. 'You're in trouble, I've no doubt.'

'How did you – ?' Sly Stoat began, then hastily added, 'Of course, you can see my agitation. My mate, the wily stoat, is sick. Her wiles were not enough to save her from the otters' revenge. What can I do?'

'Otters' revenge?' the old hedgehog repeated. He knew nothing about the trail of voles. 'No, the otters are gone. It is not revenge. It is fate. The fate of Farthing Wood and everything in it is sealed. It will not be long before the humans know this.'

Sly Stoat was puzzled and irritated. What sort of advice was this? 'I don't understand your rigmarole,' he muttered. 'All I want is for my mate to be well again.'

'A vain hope, I fear,' Sage Hedgehog replied, 'when the Wood itself is doomed.'

The sly stoat had achieved nothing and was baffled and angry. 'Why, you silly, flea-ridden old thorncoat,' he snarled and made a rush towards him.

Sage Hedgehog instantly turned himself into a pincushion and Sly Stoat, more frustrated than ever, had to abandon him.

In the makeshift shelter of their log the three otters shuddered as new, frightening sounds assaulted their ears. The thunder and clatter of passing trains rocked the ground beneath them. It was a noise so terrifying that it made them desperate to escape from that place immediately – even in the daylight. Slow Otter, who hadn't, of course, the benefit of a proper hiding-place, had run at once when the first train approached. He had made the mistake of trying to cross the track and had blundered directly into a live rail. His body was still draped over it when the train passed. There was very little of him to be seen afterwards.

In one of the lulls between trains, Sleek Otter led her companions out of the log. She drew a sharp intake of breath. 'Look,' she gasped. 'We mustn't go across there. Some poor creature has been caught and killed by the monster.'

'Where shall we go? Oh, where *can* we go?' cried Long-Whiskers who was at her wits' end.

Sleek Otter tried to keep calm. 'Away from this dangerous place at least,' she answered. She looked all round for some feature that promised a vestige of safety. There were buildings and other forbidding shapes at every point. She realized they had strayed too far into the alien world of humans.

'We must be quick,' Lame Otter urged. 'We're vulnerable in the daylight.'

'What do you suggest then?' Sleek Otter snapped, overcome by tension.

'I don't know. But we have to find shelter.'

'I know that, I know that,' she hissed. 'All right, let's try this way.' In a nearby overgrown garden, rank plants offered a hiding-place. She set off at a run, leaving the other two to follow at their own pace. Lame Otter was soon trailing behind the females.

'I shall be the next to be separated,' he muttered to himself as he thought of Slow Otter. As he limped along, a crow which had seen the dead meat on the railway track, flew close beside him, carrying part of the severed head of the unfortunate animal. Lame Otter heard the beat of wings and looked up. Slow Otter's disfigured face seemed to stare at him from the bird's coal-black beak. The crow rose higher in the air. Lame Otter squealed in horror as he recognized his old companion. He seemed to feel the full force of the hostile environment pressing in on him. The otters' attempts at survival were futile. Slow Otter had been right. It was only a matter of time before all of them succumbed to the only destiny that awaited them here – extinction. With a terrible regularity, the little party's numbers were being whittled away. Whatever they planned, wherever they went, mattered little. Their defeat, ultimately, in this uneven struggle was inevitable.

'I'm the last dog otter,' the lame male told himself. 'When I die the long history of·Farthing Wood otters will be finished.' Mechanically he continued in the wake of the two bitches. But he knew suddenly, beyond any doubt, what he must do. He must choose one of the two remaining females and return with her to the banks of the stream where they were born. For, whatever happened then, the future of the Farthing Wood otter colony wouldn't have been needlessly sacrificed before it had been given a final chance of rebirth.

11. Choices

REPORTS in the local press about strange sightings of otters and their apparent disappearance from their native habitat were not, of course, overlooked by some bodies of people who welcomed the news. While the conservationists were striving to locate and rescue the animals who had fled and endangered themselves further, these other kinds of humans were venturing into Farthing Wood to take stock for themselves.

Almost as if he had been expecting it, Sage Hedgehog saw a group of men pacing the banks of the stream, intent on acquiring the evidence they needed. Safe under a fallen branch on the edge of the Wood, the old creature watched their movements with foreboding. These men were not dressed in the way that humans who entered Farthing Wood were usually dressed. To Sage Hedgehog this implied a different human type altogether.

Later, in the gathering dusk, the men penetrated the Wood itself and passed within a metre of the hedgehog's obscuring branch. He observed them and their furtive glances for as long as they were within sight. Then, as soon as he deemed it safe to move, he scuttled in their footsteps, seeking any fellow woodlanders who would have the sense to stop and listen to him. Luckily he came across Kindly Badger who was busy digging up wild garlic root with his powerful claws.

'I count myself fortunate to have found you first,' Sage Hedgehog began in his usual verbose way, 'because, of all the animals, you are the least likely to discount my intentions.'

'Well now,' Kindly Badger said, chomping on a bulb, 'what's worrying you on this occasion?'

'Did you see them?'

'Them? Who?'

'The humans. They must have come this way only moments since.'

'Probably while I was still in my set,' the badger remarked calmly. 'The youngster thought he detected their smell.'

'They were here,' Sage Hedgehog assured him. 'I watched them for a long while.'

'That in itself is nothing out of the ordinary, is it?' Kindly Badger asked mildly. 'We've been used to humans walking –'

'No,' Sage Hedgehog interrupted sharply. 'Not this sort of human.' He was tired of the same old response.

'What do you mean? How were these different?'

'These humans have the greedy eyes and stony faces of the selfish. My friend, no good will come of their curiosity. These are not tree-gazers like the ones you refer to.'

Kindly Badger was disturbed. 'What does their presence indicate then, do you think?'

'It indicates harm,' the old hedgehog predicted. 'Harm to us and to the Wood.'

'Will you speak to others about this?' the badger asked. 'It does seem, perhaps, that this time we should take note.'

'I shall talk to the foxes,' the determined hedgehog replied. 'I have some hopes that the stout one at least may listen this time. He can help us. I shall tell him the foxes must track the otters and bring them back before it's too late!'

However some of the foxes hastily backtracked, making detours, when they saw Sage Hedgehog approaching. It was spring and they were too preoccupied with their own needs and duties to wish to bother with him. But the old creature valiantly persisted in calling for their attention. He still hoped by some means to involve them. Stout Fox failed to avoid him and was obliged to stand and listen to his latest message.

'What you say all sounds very plausible, I'm sure,' he told the hedgehog afterwards, impressed by his urgency. 'But I think it must be a long time since you had a mate carrying your young. At times like this there's very little opportunity for the father to think about anything else. I can't deal with your demands just now.' And he carried on his way. He was not yet a father, but he was soon to be so, and in the meantime Stout Vixen needed nourishing and was relying on him to provide for her.

Sage Hedgehog was fatalistic about the animals' reactions. 'They *will* listen to me,' he told himself. 'In time they will. They must. I shall continue to give warnings and try to persuade them to heed them. One day they will understand. I know my role and I shall pursue it.'

Away from the Wood, Lame Otter limped into the thick growth of grass and weeds where the two bitch otters were lying restlessly. He told them what he had seen of the dead male, and let the realization sink in of the otters' mortal vulnerability in this vicious new world. The females were silent and sombre. Lame Otter wondered who would choose to join him on his return journey. He knew it was only in that way that his partner would be decided. He was perfectly aware that, as a prospective mate, neither would choose him in normal circumstances. He waited a while. Then he spoke.

'We shall all die out here,' he said simply. 'And very soon. There is one other option. You must both know what that is.'

Long-Whiskers looked at him longingly, as if begging him to take the decision for her.

'The other option,' said Sleek Otter, 'doesn't exist as far as I'm concerned. For me there's no going back.'

Lame Otter and Long-Whiskers exchanged meaningful glances. They both understood the choice was made.

Sleek Otter understood too. After a period of silence she said quietly, 'Don't persuade me to come with you. I wish you well. But I – I shall be a lone otter with, I think, a better chance of cheating danger.' She was putting a brave face on it. They all knew that and there was nothing more to say.

At dusk the three otters moved. Their first priority was to find food. Whereas before Sleek Otter had taken the lead in exploration, Lame Otter and Long-Whiskers realized now they must rely on themselves. They deliberately took a different direction from Sleek Otter, parting from her without a word and aware, as she was, that they would never see each other again.

'You'll have to do the hunting,' Lame Otter said to his companion. 'I'm useless as a predator.'

'I know,' Long-Whiskers answered. 'I'll do my best.'

Lame Otter limped behind. Suddenly Long-Whiskers turned and said, 'It would be best if you lie low while I'm on a hunt. We need to practise stealth if we're going to eat and –'

'And I'm clumsy? Yes, I've got the foxes to thank for that,' Lame Otter interrupted bitterly. They were both at once reminded of the perils that would have to be faced back in Farthing Wood. 'I'll go back to where we left the sleek one,' he said. 'I don't know where else I can lie hidden.'

Rain began to fall heavily as he returned to the overgrown garden. The evening was cool and the grasses and wet soil smelt sweet. The shower brought frogs and toads out of hiding. The garden, long untended, had provided a perfect refuge for them. Lame Otter was exhilarated. He ignored the foul-tasting toads and pounced on a frog that squatted only a few centimetres away. This success lifted his spirits, but the frogs were able to leap considerable distances and afterwards he never quite managed to get close enough before his prey vaulted beyond reach. He longed for Long-Whiskers to return. He knew that here she could have rounded up a good meal for them in no time. The one frog he had been able to eat had tasted delicious and he was impatient for more.

'Come on, come on,' he fretted as he watched with exasperation while the frogs themselves seized their own prey in the shape of slugs and worms, although he went hungry.

Suddenly, noiselessly, Long-Whiskers was beside him. She had brought no food. 'Quickly, come *now*,' she whispered. 'I ran into some humans and only escaped in the nick of time.' She was quivering with fright. 'One tried to grab me. They're after us – they're carrying traps and bright gleaming lights that shine all around like huge stars.'

'But-but,' Lame Otter stammered, looking at the frogs with regret, 'there's food here. Can't we hide?'

'Not here,' she hissed. Even as she spoke Lame Otter heard human voices, and abruptly the garden was swept by powerful torch-light. Long-Whiskers leapt in alarm and raced away.

'There it is!' a man cried, seeing her movement.

'There's another!' came a second voice as Lame Otter was bathed in light, cowering back amongst the greenery.

The men came crashing into the garden, intent on capturing the animals they had been seeking for days. Fear clawed at Lame Otter's heart and lent speed to his limbs. A net was thrown at him, but he dodged it and scrambled clear, running as he had never run since receiving his wound. He was oblivious of any pain; his injured leg seemed to respond to his desperate need to escape.

'Catch it!', 'Stop it!' human voices cried as the men thrashed about, trying another throw of the net. But Lame Otter had found darkness again and, using its merciful veil, he raced away as though all the foxes in Farthing Wood were after him.

Long-Whiskers had run towards the railway embankment. She could think only of the deep black interior of the hollow log and wanted to wrap herself in its protection again. Her fur streamed with water. She took great gulps of air as she ran, straining every muscle to reach her goal. But, before she could find sanctuary, a train – a monster of speed and light – came rushing, as she thought, towards her out of the gloom. She reared up, changing tack, and ran along the crest of the embankment, parallel to the railway line. The train disappeared. Long-Whiskers continued to run blindly. The embankment dropped down to a road which crossed the line at that point. A few cars were crawling over this level crossing. The barriers had just been raised following the passing of the train. Long-Whiskers slowed and hesitated. She seemed to recognize the road as the way to escape the rushing monsters. She pattered across the line in the wake of the vehicles and then veered away through an orchard that bordered the embankment on the opposite side.

Lame Otter had seen her dark shape illuminated on the crest by the lights from the train windows, and he struggled to keep her in view. He was so fearful of losing her, with all that would entail, that the shock of the humans' sudden appearance became of secondary consideration. He trailed her to the level crossing and then, on the other side, could find no trace of where she had gone next. He called her urgently.

Long-Whiskers had paused to draw breath. His plaintive cries reached her ears. Joyfully, and with relief, she answered. Lame Otter hobbled towards her. Now that the immediate danger was averted, pain reclaimed his senses and his pace became agonizingly slow. She was waiting for him under an apple tree whose boughs were awash with blossom.

'Brave creature,' she breathed compassionately. 'You saved yourself.'

'At some ... cost ... I'm afraid,' Lame Otter gasped.

'We've escaped them for now,' Long-Whiskers resumed. 'But they won't give us up if they think we're still in the area.'

'Then we ... must leave it.'

'Tomorrow. You can go no further for the present.'

'No.'

'Rest here while I look for a refuge.'

'Don't go far,' he pleaded.

'Only as far as is necessary,' she assured him.

Lame Otter collapsed against the trunk of the apple-tree. His legs trembled violently from his exertions. He wondered if he would even be able to move as far as the nearest hiding-place. No human sounds were evident and he fell into a sleep of exhaustion.

He was wakened by Long-Whiskers' gentle nudges. It was a while before he could recover himself and recognize what was happening.

'Some luck at last,' she was murmuring. 'I've found a pond in the next field. There's plenty of cover and there are water-fowl and a moorhen's nest. We can take shelter and feed ourselves at the same time. There's nothing like the savour of tender young nestlings.'

Lame Otter looked at her dreamily. 'I have a feeling,' he said, 'things are about to change for us.'

12. Another Victim

THE OTTER pair hid themselves thankfully amongst a thick growth of water-irises. How could they know that the humans they had evaded meant them no harm? That they actually would have delivered them to their old home by a much safer and quicker route? To the animals, these men with their brilliant lamps and their nets seemed terrifying. As for Sleek Otter, she had bolted into a drainage ditch where she lay quaking until the humans had disappeared.

Meanwhile Farthing Wood held its breath. Nervous Squirrel's agitated cries of 'S-strangers in the Wood' were heard more frequently. The tranquillity of the woodland was disturbed regularly by the cold, calculating humans whom Sage Hedgehog had first witnessed. They took a particular interest in the grassland surrounding the Wood, returning to it at intervals, and giving the appearance that they were in their clever way taking its measure.

'Too close for comfort,' Jay screamed as he flew overhead. And the Wood's inhabitants trod warily and quietly until they were left alone again.

Lean Fox said to his vixen, 'The Wood is uneasy. Every creature is on tenterhooks. Sickness is rife and men come spying. Things were less fraught when the otters were here.'

'How can you say that?' Lean Vixen rounded on him. 'There was constant friction. At least these men don't steal our food. We're of no interest to them at all.'

'I think you're mistaken,' Lean Fox said quietly. 'If we're of no interest, why do they continue to return here?'

'Who knows? Who cares? As long as we can hunt and keep our cubs free from sickness, that's all we need to concern ourselves about.'

The sickness was spreading, claiming more victims. Quick Weasel and Wily Stoat had died and other animals throughout the Wood were now suffering. For some creatures it became increasingly difficult to know where to hunt and what areas to shun.

Stout Vixen, whose cubs would soon be born, saw her mate arrive from his foraging with nothing.

'How can you come into our earth carrying nothing?' she berated him. 'This is the second occasion. Perhaps I should hunt for myself?'

'You certainly have the greater skill,' Stout Fox replied magnanimously. 'Believe me, I've tried everywhere. The rabbits are becoming much more wary and you know I don't like settling for other prey. It's particularly risky with some of them carrying disease.'

'I understand your motives,' the vixen said. 'But what are we to do? If you can no longer catch a rabbit, then you must look elsewhere.'

'I've done so,' he replied. 'Would you want me to bring you beetles and moths?'

'Well, I must eat,' Stout Vixen said. 'Fasting at a time like this is unacceptable.' She stood up. 'Is the Wood quiet?'

'Quiet and still.'

'I'll find something, I've no doubt,' she declared with confidence.

Stout Fox followed her through the exit hole. A shower of rain pattered through the leafy trees.

'I'll go alone,' Stout Vixen told him. 'Perhaps I'll find something.'

Stout Fox said admiringly, 'If anyone can, *you* will do so.'

Stout Vixen trotted beneath the trees towards the stream. She had a feeling that some kind of quarry might be sheltering there, enjoying a period of prosperity in the otters' absence. 'How many have hunted here,' she wondered to herself, 'since those animals left?' Almost at once she flushed a water-vole from the bank. It plopped into the water, but the vixen's eager jaws snatched it and crushed it in one swift lunge.

'There are more of you around somewhere,' she said after she had eaten. She paddled into the stream, nosing her way amongst the reeds. A pair of coots scuttled out of her reach, calling in alarm and leaving their neat nest exposed with four unhatched eggs just waiting to be devoured.

'Haven't tasted eggs in an age,' Stout Vixen murmured to herself. She cracked one open with her strong teeth and licked at the succulent contents. She chuckled to herself. 'It doesn't seem right, all this for me while my mate goes hungry.' She smacked her lips and broke another egg. 'They really are delicious.' When there was only one left, her conscience smote her. 'I'll carry this back for the fox,' she murmured. 'He's faithfully tried his best on my behalf.' She picked it up carefully and set off.

On the edge of the woodland she surprised a bank vole. Instinct got the better of her. She dropped the egg, which broke, and pursued the rodent. She was keen to prove to herself she had lost none of her speed. She cornered the vole, killed it, then checked herself.

'Do I eat it?' she wondered. She sniffed at the body. 'Hm. Nothing wrong with *that*. Can't afford to waste anything.' She gobbled it down, then noticed the broken egg. 'Ah well, as I said . . .'

'*Stop!*'

She turned, startled. Stout Fox, who had been searching for her, had seen the kill and was anxious no vole should be eaten in that quarter.

'You?' Stout Vixen said. 'Why did you cry out? It's only an egg.'

'You can eat that and welcome to it. Where's your kill?'

Stout Vixen was puzzled. 'Kill?'

'The vole!'

'You saw me? Was I fast?'

'Yes, as fast as ever. Where *is* it?'

'Well, I've eaten it, of course.'

Stout Fox slumped. 'How could you? After all I've said? I've been so careful, taken such pains . . .'

'All right, all right,' she told him, but now a little worried. 'There was nothing wrong with it. It smelt good.'

'Smelt?' he repeated faintly. 'How on earth did you think it would smell? You can't tell by their odour.'

Stout Vixen gaped. Her stomach lurched. 'It looked healthy.'

'How can we be sure?' Stout Fox demanded. 'Wouldn't it be better to avoid this kind of prey until we know it's safe?'

The vixen felt some relief. 'So you're not sure either,' she retorted. 'Why do you try to scare me?'

'I don't wish to. I'm only concerned for your well-being. And for your litter.'

Stout Vixen softened. 'You're a good partner. I've grown used to you and I like your company. Look – I was carrying this egg for you. Won't you try it?'

'Of course I'll try it,' Stout Fox grunted. 'I've eaten nothing at all!' He quickly demolished the egg's contents. 'Are there more?' He looked at her with hungry eyes.

'Er – no. I don't think so,' the vixen answered evasively. 'Are you going to hunt again?'

'I'll see what I can pick up for myself.'

'Good. I shall return to the den. And I feel perfectly all right, so don't vex yourself about that vole.'

*

Far away from Farthing Wood, Sleek Otter
was feeling very alone. From the drainage
ditch she had travelled swiftly and always
directly away from the place where she had
dived for cover from the humans. She knew
that wherever she found to rest at the end of
that day, for the first time she would have no
company. It was a chilling thought, but she
had made her choice and there was no going
back.

The dark hours were kind to her. There
were no further alarms. When daylight came
she looked around in amazement. The entire
countryside seemed to have been swallowed
up by forbidding patterns of brick, stone,
metal and asphalt. These spread before her in
a bewildering mosaic which puzzled and
frightened her. Behind her was the countryside
through which she had just run. She knew she
had to go forward, but where? And how?

'This can be no home,' she acknowledged
to herself. 'I can't hide in there.' A sudden

noise made her jump. An aeroplane droned across the sky, high up, like a monstrous silver bee. A starling flitted over the house-tops and perched on a television aerial. Sleek Otter was impressed by the bird's adaptability. 'Perhaps there is some shelter somewhere for me after all,' she sighed.

She crossed an empty road and padded along a pavement, looking for an opening between the looming buildings. A cat sitting on a wall arched its back and hissed at the strange beast. The cat was just as strange to the otter and she scampered away. In the distance a milk-float approached with a rattle of milk-crates and clinking of bottles. Sleek Otter was bombarded by new sounds and crushed by an unyielding environment. There were no trees, no streams, no rushes, no reeds. And no food. The town was a nightmare for a vulnerable, solitary and ravenous wild creature.

'I've no chance here,' Sleek Otter told herself. 'I might as well have been taken by the humans.' Then suddenly she saw a gap. As the milkman came nearer she bolted down an alley between two blocks of flats. There was no greenery, no plant growth to hide in. It was a cul de sac, leading to a row of garages. Sleek Otter found she was in a dead end. One garage, however, had been opened. The door had been pushed up and the garage's dark interior seemed her only refuge. She ran inside. It was dusty and dry, but in one corner a clutter of cartons offered some protection. She tried to hide herself amongst them and, thoroughly weary, fell asleep.

Later in the morning there was much activity. Many people were collecting their cars to drive to work or to take children to school. Sleek Otter awoke to the din of revving engines, slamming doors and loud human voices. She dared not move. Yet as car after car rumbled past her place of concealment, she caught the acrid smell of petrol fumes which steadily threatened to choke her. At last she couldn't remain still. She dashed from the garage, almost colliding with some schoolchildren.

'Look, Daddy! What's that? It's . . . it's . . . '

'An otter!' cried the father. 'How on earth . . . ?'

The children rushed at the animal, eager to save it from danger. But Sleek Otter slipped past them and, in sheer terror, bolted for the alley. As she neared it a car, reversing from the first garage in the block, hit her and rolled backwards over her. The children screamed out but it was too late. Their father grabbed them as they tried to run forward.

'It's no good, children. We can't do anything,' he told them regretfully. 'Poor creature. Wherever could it have come from? It must have been someone's pet.'

The driver of the vehicle had felt a bump and got out to investigate. It was a young woman who was really distressed by what she found.

'Oh no, not another one,' she wailed. 'They seem to be bent on destroying themselves.'

The father asked her to explain.

'Haven't you heard? There has been a spate of accidents recently involving otters. They've been run over, drowned, killed by dogs. It's all very strange and very upsetting. Such lovely animals too . . . '

'How sad,' the man commented. 'They must be rarities in these parts.'

13. The Last of the Otters

STOUT Vixen was certain she had suffered no ill effects from eating the vole. She felt no different.

'You were lucky,' her mate told her.

'No, I don't think so. Probably all the voles with disease have perished or been accounted for by now.'

'Maybe. But don't forget – it only takes one.'

Stout Vixen thought her mate was being over-cautious. She determined that, if he couldn't feed her properly in these last crucial days, she would supplement her diet from the banned area where now no fox nor other predator hunted. 'But I shan't tell him,' she chuckled to herself. 'He gets in such a stew about it.'

Farthing Wood and all it represented was drawing Lame Otter and Long-Whiskers steadily towards it. They had eaten well by the pond and were in good spirits as they continued homewards.

'Do you think we can reach our stream easily?' Long-Whiskers asked her companion who now, also, had become her mate. 'Or will we always be in danger?'

'We must take every precaution,' the dog otter replied. 'And, regretfully, my company will make the journey slower and seem longer than it would be if you were on your own.'

'But I wouldn't be making it on my own,' she assured him gently.

'Well then, we are content.' Lame Otter limped by her side. He tried not to think about what would happen to the other if one of them met with an accident. 'We must aim for the Metal Ponds where we caught all those fish. If we find our way there without trouble, we should be over the worst.'

'Do you ever think about the foxes?' Long-Whiskers asked.

'Sometimes. I have cause enough,' Lame Otter answered, remembering the fight that had disabled him.

'Perhaps if we steal into our holt by the stream quietly, no one will know we're there.'

'Did you have a den?'

'Yes. Where I was born.'

'Are you attached to it?'

'I suppose so. Did you have a different plan?'

'No. I shall be happy where you're happy. And your comfort must be paramount.'

'Thank you. My holt is a snug home for cubs.'

They fell silent, full of thoughts of a new generation of Farthing Wood otters. They didn't reach the trout farm that night. Lame Otter's leg was painful and Long-Whiskers persuaded him to rest. They took shelter in a rabbit burrow, intending to move on the next night. The rabbits panicked as the otters entered the warren. Most of them took flight, but Long-Whiskers pounced on a youngster who hesitated, and she and her mate enjoyed a feast.

'Will we ever eat fish again?' Long-Whiskers sighed.

The same thought had occurred to Lame Otter. But he said, 'As long as we eat. That's all we can hope for at present.'

They slept during the daylight hours and at dusk the next day, fully refreshed, they set off again. Lame Otter's spirits were buoyant. 'You know, I've had a feeling of confidence since we made our decision,' he told his companion. 'I'm sure everything is going to work out for us. It's as though we have earned our right to survive because we're the last

Farthing Wood otters. We *have* to do so for the sake of the rest of them.'

Long-Whiskers was encouraged by his words. Neither of them had spoken of Sleek Otter. Now Long-Whiskers said, 'You really believe we are the last now?'

'There can't be any doubt, can there? There never was any chance of any of us living permanently out here. I have realized that for a long time.'

In the middle of the night they caught sight of the trout lake and the buildings around the trout farm. Lame Otter let out a whistle of delight. 'There!' he cried joyfully. 'That's our landmark. The most dangerous part is over for us. We're almost home. Come on, we can have a swim!'

They loped to the lake and dived in gratefully. Their delight in swimming made them a little reckless, and they were still happily playing in the water when dawn broke. Their antics were spotted by the very dog that had killed one of their old companions. The animal yelped excitedly outside its kennel, fetching its owner, who had then scarcely stepped out of bed, hurrying down to quieten it. It wasn't long before the man discovered the reason for his dog's outburst. He watched the otter pair for a while through binoculars, and then went to telephone a friend who was an enthusiastic member of the local Wildlife Trust. In very little time a party was assembled and on the move to the trout farm. It was hoped that on this occasion, finally, a capture would successfully be made.

The otters' sport came abruptly to an end when they heard the dog bark. They submerged and paddled along the lake bottom. Lame Otter broke the surface briefly to keep a look-out. The dog had disappeared by then. The otters left the lake hurriedly while the coast was clear. All this was noted by the dog's owner. He took care to follow their direction so that he could give the appropriate advice.

Naturally the conservationists' plan was to head the animals off.

Lame Otter and Long-Whiskers ran across country. They remembered the hedgerow where they had hidden with their five companions, and hoped to take shelter there again. As they ran, a Land-Rover entered a field ahead of them, stopped suddenly and disgorged a handful of eager people. The people came quickly towards them, pointing and gesticulating. The otters knew only too well what this meant. This time there were no brilliant lights but the animals hadn't forgotten the terrifying experience near the railway line. They turned instinctively and ran back towards the lake, the only place now where they knew they could hide themselves. Lame Otter lagged behind. He gasped, 'Save yourself! Don't wait for me.'

Long-Whiskers looked back. The men were closer. With extreme anguish she forced herself to abandon him. She knew she must survive now at all costs if the Farthing Wood race of otters was not to be extinguished forever. All at once her sharp eyes saw a burrow entrance in the corner of the field under a group of trees. She called excitedly. 'Here! Here! We're saved.' She had no idea this was the entrance to a badger set, and not a rabbit burrow.

Lame Otter made a supreme effort as he saw the hole. Long-Whiskers vanished inside as he laboured to make his escape. The humans were almost close enough to grab him. He heard their thudding footsteps and their quick breathing. A shadow began to envelop him. He remembered the nets. He dived for safety. The darkness of the tunnel enclosed him. He smelt not the smell of rabbit, but of badger. And then, ahead, a violent commotion broke out. Long-Whiskers had run straight into the sow badger's nursery chamber where her new-born young were suckling. The badger reared up angrily to protect her cubs from the intruder. She lashed out at Long-Whiskers with her powerful claws and lunged at the smaller animal with her sharp teeth. At this season the mother badger had a fierce nature, her one imperative being to raise and defend her young. Long-Whiskers backed away. She was wounded, but not severely. The badger sow launched another attack, this time with the purpose of killing the otter who posed such a threat to her litter.

Now Lame Otter came into the fray, in his turn trying to defend his mate. The badger, furious at the sight of a second intruder, called up reinforcements from elsewhere in the set. A tremendous and vicious battle began. The otters were outnumbered and outmatched in power and strength. They had no chance.

Outside the set the group of people heard the furious growlings and roarings of the badgers and the shrieks and yelps of the injured otters. They knew only too well what the outcome of such an uneven contest would be. They waited vainly for the otters to retreat up the tunnel. Retreat was their only hope of avoiding certain death. Gradually the angry snarls subsided into silence. Even then the human onlookers continued to wait. None of them spoke. Each felt that their well-meant plans to save the otters and return them to their rightful home had somehow been blighted. Every one of their attempts to help had backfired. Sadly they had put the animals into greater jeopardy by their good intentions.

One man said, 'Another failure. No otter could come out of there alive. Not from a badger's set in the breeding season.'

A woman said, 'We must wait a bit. Just in case . . . ' But she herself knew that the otters had been slain. It was inconceivable that their presence in the set would be tolerated.

'Were these the last two?' another man asked.

'Probably,' said the first man. 'The other female was killed by a car. There have been no other reports.'

'Then we've all lost.'

'It looks like it.'

Wearily and miserably the party trudged back to their vehicle. Each of them was only too aware what might result from the permanent loss of an otter population in Farthing Wood. They didn't voice their thoughts. They were too dejected. They climbed into the Land-Rover quietly, avoiding each other's glances. Soon the field was empty again.

Following this incident, the local press printed a report from the Wildlife Trust about its fear that the last of the Farthing Wood otters had perished. A description of their unfortunate demise as a result of entering a badgers' set was given. No further sightings of otters had been made in the area. It was therefore regretfully to be assumed that no other animals still survived.

14. By the Great Beech

FOR A brief period Farthing Wood seemed to breathe more freely. Sickness was on the wane. Nervous Squirrel was quiet. The animals were left to themselves. Then, abruptly, the peaceful atmosphere was shattered. Outside the Wood and beyond the stream, on the surrounding grassland, there was much activity. Men arrived with machines and tools and began to cut a swathe through the tall grasses. In no time they had made a wide, straight path which Jay, from a high perch, could see stretched back from the hinterland towards the area whence they all knew the humans came.

'A trail!' he screeched. 'A human trail in the grass!'

The animals heard and Nervous Squirrel bounded to the top of an ash tree. 'M-many strangers!' he called, flicking his tail in extreme excitement. 'B-busy strangers!'

Sage Hedgehog knew without going to investigate that the moment he had dreaded had come. The humans were too far away for his old eyes to perceive that they were building a road to give them easy access to the centre of their interest. But he shook his head over his fellow woodlanders' refusal to comprehend the perils which he had warned about.

'Such foolhardy blindness,' he muttered. 'Now their eyes will be opened.' He left his roost and went to see how the other animals were coping with the revelation. He expected to see signs that at last Farthing Wood was reacting to the danger now only too evident on its doorstep. Once again the community surprised him. The animals appeared to be continuing with their usual habits and movements, regardless of any new development. He found another hedgehog contentedly munching some grubs dug from a piece of rotten wood.

'Didn't you hear the cry from the tree-tops?' the old creature asked, amazed by the hedgehog's placidity.

'Of course I did. Isn't that silly squirrel forever calling some message or other? Such an irritating animal!'

'Well, he has something to call *about* now, doesn't he?' snapped Sage Hedgehog, annoyed by the other's lack of concern.

'What's so different about this time?'

'Do you need me to explain? The humans have come to stay.'

The younger hedgehog looked less assured suddenly. 'To stay? Where?' he asked faintly.

'Too close to *us*. They're busy in the grassy area.'

'The grassland? Oh, that's too far from here to worry about,' said the younger animal. 'It's hours of travelling.' And of course, to a hedgehog it was. 'Would you like a share of these fat larvae? They're very tasty.'

'Food is of no consequence in the circumstances,' Sage Hedgehog replied sourly and turned his back on the heedless animal.

Sly Stoat watched the approach of the ancient hedgehog prophet and quickly hid behind the trunk of a tall oak. But he wasn't quick enough. Sage Hedgehog saw movement.

'Why try to avoid me? What are you afraid of? That I might speak the truth?'

Sly Stoat muttered out of earshot, 'Afraid of? More bad news, I suppose.' Despite his mate's death, because of the decline in the numbers of sick animals in the Wood Sly Stoat was of the opinion that the otters' revenge had run its course. He slipped into the open.

'Come on, you old doom-carrier, what have you for us this time?'

'Nothing for you,' Sage Hedgehog answered primly. 'I wouldn't waste my breath. I'm on my way to talk with the more intelligent members of the community.'

'The foxes? Ha! They're too wrapped up in fetching and carrying for their mates. Don't you know, families take up a lot of time?'

'I've heard such words from others before,' Sage Hedgehog replied wearily. 'Almost the same words. And I can assure you I know all there is to know about young and their needs and demands. I wasn't always old. But now that I *am* old I have the time to look beyond such immediate concerns where perhaps others haven't. I love this place and I shall continue to do all I can to persuade others that it's vital that we *all* think about ways of saving it.'

Sly Stoat was humbled. 'I'm sorry,' he said. 'We sometimes don't give you the credit you deserve. We should recognize your warnings are driven by the care you have for Farthing Wood. A care we all, of course, share in our own way. Yet is there so very much to concern ourselves with? The sickness has abated and, so far as human presence goes, none of us, I'm sure, will be so foolish as to venture anywhere near the grassland while they're there.'

'So you do know of their presence?'

'The squirrel sees to that, doesn't he?'

Sage Hedgehog was silent for a while and he looked at Sly Stoat pensively. It was evident to him that the stoat, like the young hedgehog, couldn't see beyond the present. Perhaps only he himself had that ability. He sighed. 'Are there none of you far-sighted enough to make plans for the future?' he murmured. But Sly Stoat had already reverted to thinking about his empty stomach. He fidgeted, impatient to be off. Sage Hedgehog left him to his own devices.

The badgers were ready to talk. Kindly Badger realized something needed to be done. 'Human activity is always worrying,' he said. 'I fear for my youngsters. They won't grow up in a Wood free from interference as I and my mate did.'

'I am so thankful to have your attention,' the old hedgehog said. 'The stout fox understands my fears but is too engrossed in domestic affairs to act on them.'

'What can we do?' asked the badger.

'We have to make plans. We can't continue to believe our lives will remain unaffected.'

'We're powerless to alter the course of any human plans,' said Kindly Badger, shaking his head. 'What plans can we make?'

'You're a thoughtful animal and your size makes you more likely to be respected than I,' Sage Hedgehog told him. 'You can perhaps make the others understand they have to think about the future, even if our generation will complete its cycle without tragedy. They *must* do this for the sake of their youngsters and those still to come.'

'I think I follow your reasoning,' Kindly Badger remarked. Sage Hedgehog's words were, as always, difficult to interpret for ordinary beasts such as himself who hadn't the gift of prophecy. The old hedgehog seemed often to be on a kind of higher plane. 'I'll discuss everything with my mate,' the badger resumed. 'The sow badger is such a comfort to me. We'll try to find a way of involving all the woodlanders.'

Sage Hedgehog nodded. He thought there was very little more he could hope to achieve for the moment. 'I'm grateful to you,' he said. 'And I trust that others, too, will have cause to be so before long.'

Over the next few days the lives of the Farthing Wood animals were punctuated at regular intervals by cries from Jay or Nervous Squirrel reporting human developments.

'A wide path with machines!' shrieked Jay.

'More and m-more humans,' chattered Nervous Squirrel.

'Grass going bit by bit,' Jay called.

'B-busy humans making m-mud,' Nervous Squirrel cried.

The animals paused and tensed each time they heard a cry. Those in their daytime dens huddled closer for a while. The distant hum of human endeavour – engines, voices – droned constantly in daylight hours. For most of the animals, it was too faint to bother them unduly. Kindly Badger began to wonder what would happen if the grassland disappeared.

'The rabbits will move closer to the Wood,' the sow badger remarked. 'As the hares have done.'

'Which means the humans will have done so too,' Young Badger pointed out shrewdly.

'Quite right, my son,' the kindly old boar said. 'And then we shall all feel as if they're spying on us. Life won't be very comfortable for the birds and beasts who are around in the daytime.'

'Let them worry about that,' his mate suggested.

'I don't know. We're all together in this in a way. It's our Wood we're talking about. We all live here. I'd like to get the opinions of some other animals. We ought to do *something*.'

'What? What can we do?'

'Well, think about protecting ourselves as best we can. You know, keeping our secrecy as wild animals, and simply maintaining our natural behaviour. Humans can be very inquisitive and disruptive.'

'What shall we do, Father?' asked Young Badger.

'I think we need to get together with the other senior animals – as many as we can persuade – and talk things over. We could meet any night in the centre of the Wood – somewhere that's a good gathering place.'

'Everyone knows where the middle of the Wood is,' the sow badger said. 'By the Great Beech.'

'It'll be difficult to get the smaller animals to come along,' Kindly Badger reflected. 'They won't feel safe unless they're given a kind of promise.'

'Well then, give them one.'

Kindly Badger fell to thinking. 'It'll need the foxes' co-operation,' he murmured, 'and that's not an easy thing to arrange.'

So it was to prove. Lean Vixen scoffed at the notion of a promise. 'An absurd idea,' she said. 'To think that foxes would commit themselves in any such way. If you want to have a meeting – fine. But let everyone come at his or her own risk.'

'The badger's not so silly,' Lean Fox disagreed as he often did. 'We should have as many wise heads as we can get. Some of the smaller animals, such as the weasels and stoats, have a kind of cunning all their own. I, for one, would be willing to listen to them. They may have ideas that would be useful for all of us. I would promise to leave them unmolested.'

'And the squirrels and rabbits?' Lean Vixen mocked him. 'You'd give them a promise of safety?' She gave a hollow laugh.

'Why not?' Kindly Badger asked. 'For just the duration of our meeting?'

'They wouldn't come!' Lean Vixen protested.

'That's up to them. The squirrels might well do so. They could sit in the branches.'

'When do you propose to meet?' Lean Fox asked.

'The sooner the better. There will soon be a new moon. The darkest night is our best security. We should choose then, I think.'

'By the Great Beech?'

'Exactly. I shall invite as many woodlanders as I can find.'

'I'll speak to the stout fox,' his lean counterpart offered. 'I think he'll attend. He has been going around with a very worried look recently.'

'Oh, that's nothing to do with any human presence,' the vixen informed him glibly. 'His mate's ill and she's almost reached her time. No wonder he's worried.'

'Nevertheless . . . '

'The old hedgehog will join you,' said Lean Vixen.

'You can be sure of that. He wouldn't miss any opportunity to regale everyone with his weird fantasies.'

Stout Fox had begun to view the humans' incursions with misgiving. His own cubs would soon enter the world in the shadow of their presence, and who could say how things would develop? But his concern for his unborn cubs was overridden by a much more profound concern for his mate. Stout Vixen was very sick indeed and the big fox ran in and out of their den, unable to rest for a moment. He was at his wits' end.

'There must be something I can do,' he would mutter. 'I can't just let her suffer.' Inside the earth he looked longingly at her. 'Poor vixen! Are you in great pain?'

'Pretty much,' she whispered.

'If only I could help,' Stout Fox moaned.

'But you can't . . . we both know that.'

'Perhaps there is a creature somewhere . . . ' he murmured and broke off as he heard a voice outside.

Lean Fox had come to give news of the meeting. Stout Fox scarcely listened, his mind was so taken up with his mate's illness.

'The Great Beech, you say? All right, I'll come.' Then a thought struck him. Maybe one of the animals at the meeting could offer some hope. He called after Lean Fox as he left. 'I'll certainly attend. As long as it's safe to leave my vixen . . . '

The night of the new moon arrived. Kindly Badger and his mate, along with various hedgehogs, Lean Fox and Lean Vixen, sat waiting beneath the Great Beech. Sly Stoat,

Lightning Weasel, and others of their kind, came cautiously. In the branches of the beech Nervous Squirrel and others perched restlessly. A pair of hares, who trusted the badger's word, had come to listen to the discussion from a safe distance. Other smaller animals peeped from holes nearby. And various birds clustered in the tree-tops, alert to every movement.

Jay spied Stout Fox loping through the Wood to its centre. 'The stout fox is coming!' the bird screeched, putting several timid beasts to flight at once.

'Come back, come back,' Kindly Badger called. 'There's no danger. Everyone assembled here must take the Oath of Common Safety, so that none can be harmed. Otherwise there will be no exchange of views and no opinions heard.'

Stout Fox appeared out of the gloom. He was the largest animal present. 'I swear,' he growled, looking around the gathering, 'to respect the safety of all creatures assembled for this meeting.'

Others followed suit. It was a solemn moment.

Stout Fox mumbled in a low voice, 'My vixen is sick. She must have found the last diseased vole. There has been no other sickness for days. Does anyone know of a creature who has survived the sickness?'

No one answered.

'I must save her if I can,' the fox continued. It was strange to see the powerful hunter wearing a look of helplessness. 'She will bear our cubs very soon. She mustn't die. Not yet.' It was as though he were talking to himself.

'Some of the otters cured themselves,' Sage Hedgehog said when the fox fell quiet. 'They had the knowledge. But you drove them away. They are not here to help you now.'

Stout Fox hung his head in misery.

'I thought this assembly was all about protecting ourselves from human interference,'

Sly Stoat interposed drily. 'Much as the stout vixen has everyone's sympathy, we really have to think of what concerns us all.' His sarcasm was evident, but none of the smaller animals dared to acknowledge it.

'Well, it doesn't concern *me*,' Lean Vixen announced, 'if you're referring to the humans' activities. I don't hunt in the grassy area any more. I don't need to. There are plenty of other places to find all the game *I* want. And I can't believe anyone here is so stupid as to go nosing around that quarter these days. Let the humans attend to their interests, whatever they are, and leave me to attend to mine.'

'A more shortsighted remark would be difficult to utter,' Kindly Badger retorted, angry for once. 'I wonder you came along.'

'She's fully occupied with our cubs, you see,' Lean Fox tried to excuse her. 'She can't think of anything else.'

'Perhaps she'd better return to them, then, and leave us to the serious discussion.'

'An argument!' Jay shrieked. 'Not a good start!'

'But the vixen's right,' Lightning Weasel gave his opinion. 'We don't have to watch the humans' every move. We can forget them, at any rate for the foreseeable future. They're too far away to cause us any concern.'

'M-moving nearer, I think,' Nervous Squirrel said. 'I w-watch them. They s-seem to creep closer each time I l-look.'

'You're imagining it,' the weasel replied. 'How can you tell?'

'Why don't you look for yourself?' Sly Stoat sneered. 'Then you'll know!'

'I can't climb into tree-tops,' Lightning Weasel snapped.

'I think we're losing sight of why we're here,' Kindly Badger interrupted.

'Why are we here?' Lightning Weasel chortled, glancing around.

Kindly Badger sighed. 'In your case – and in some others – it would be difficult to say.

But I called this assembly so that all of us can air our views as to how to proceed in these difficult times.'

'What's he talking about?' one hare muttered to the other.

'I don't know. Waste of time coming, if you ask me.'

Lean Vixen cut across the mutterings. 'There is nothing anyone here can do to put things right.' She looked serious for once. 'That's if you believe things have gone wrong in the first place. We drove the otters out. We have more to eat, but the humans seem to have replaced the otters. That's the story in as few words as it takes to tell.'

'And what of your cubs' future?' Sage Hedgehog asked her. 'How do you propose to protect them?'

'The same way my parents protected me,' she answered. 'Nothing has altered that. And when they no longer need me, well . . . they're on their own.'

These words seemed to summarize the situation for every creature present. Beyond usual parental duties, there *was* nothing more in their power to do. The meeting began to break up without reaching any agreement. The smaller animals left first. And gradually all of the beasts and birds returned to their homes or their normal occupations in the night hours. Kindly Badger and Sage Hedgehog were left alone under the Great Beech.

'They are beyond redemption,' the hedgehog said with finality.

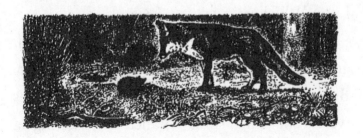

15. Stout Fox's Quest

FAR AWAY from Farthing Wood another group of badgers were tidying their set after their fight with the intruding otters. It had been a short and savage fight. The mother badger watched her mate take the lifeless form of Lame Otter by the scruff of the neck and carry it along the entrance tunnel to the outside air. Lame Otter had borne the brunt of the attack as he had tried to shield Long-Whiskers. His wounds were ghastly. The badger dropped him far enough from the set so that no taint could foul the air of the nesting chamber. Then he returned for Long-Whiskers.

The badgers believed both otters were dead, and indeed Lame Otter was at his last gasp. But, severe though Long-Whiskers' injuries were, she had some chance of making a recovery. She was dropped by the side of Lame Otter. The badger returned to his set, satisfied that the intruders had been properly dealt with.

Long-Whiskers opened her eyes. It was still light. She knew she must somehow crawl away from that place before dusk, because then the badgers would leave the set to forage. If they should discover she was still alive, they would quickly finish her off. She sniffed at the still body of the lame male.

'Are you lost to me?' she whispered. The horrible ache of loneliness had not yet made itself felt. Pain and fear dominated her senses. She detected the tiniest flicker of movement in her companion as he struggled to draw a breath.

'You're still living!' she whistled softly, though aware life was ebbing from him.

Barely audibly Lame Otter gasped, 'Leave here. Go on. You ... must get back.' The effort exhausted him, but he tried to speak again. 'You ... the last. For the cubs ... ' These were his last words. He shuddered and was then quite still.

For a while Long-Whiskers remained loyally by his side. Then, for his sake as well as for her own, she began to crawl away. She had lost a lot of blood and she felt weak and sick. Her gashes were extremely painful. Amazingly, though, her limbs were still sound. The badgers' attack had been directed against her chest and head. She paused after dragging herself a metre or two; then continued. She knew she couldn't rest just yet. Little by little she removed herself from the scene of that horrible encounter, so that by dusk she was able to haul herself under a hedgerow, secure in the knowledge that she had escaped the badgers. She slept the deep sleep of exhaustion; helpless, injured and totally alone.

The grassland around Farthing Wood shrank steadily as the human construction site began to take shape. The Farthing Wood animals, for the most part, tried to ignore the fact. But some of them recalled the otters' boasts. They remembered how there had, in truth, been no human activity when the otters lived by the stream. And they remembered how the foxes and others had plotted to rid themselves of the clever animals, and, in particular, that the foxes had joined together to drive the otters out. Rabbits and hares had already lost their chosen homes in the grassy areas they loved best. Some of the more thoughtful animals wondered now if that was only the start.

'Do you think that our set will always be here?' Young Badger asked his father one day.

'Of course it will,' Kindly Badger replied at once. 'Why, generation after generation of badgers have been born and raised here. It's – it's – *unthinkable* that that could ever change.' He glanced at his mate for corroboration, as though perhaps needing reassurance himself.

'Don't worry,' she said softly to the youngster. 'You'll grow old here, of that I'm quite sure.'

The young male couldn't think beyond that point and was happy.

The foxes didn't worry themselves about past events. The otters had gone and they thought that was a good thing. Yet Stout Fox would have been prepared to humble himself and ask an otter's advice about the sickness of his vixen if an otter had been around for him to do so.

Stout Vixen lay listlessly in their earth. She regretted her failure to be guided by her mate and to shun any voles as food. She hadn't cared for his over-protection. But he had been right. The sickness had taken hold of her and wouldn't go away. Each day she felt a little worse. She tried to eat what little Stout Fox brought her, so that at least she would have the strength to bring her cubs into the world when the time came. But gradually she came to realize that the cubs might be infected too, even if disease didn't claim her before they had a chance of life.

Stout Fox was beside himself with worry. There was no creature he could consult who had the secret of the cure. He watched the vixen wilt and sink a little more with every dawn. In desperation he set off through the Wood one evening in quest of Sage Hedgehog. As he went he told himself it was unlikely that the hedgehog could be of real assistance, but even if the old creature should offer one grain of comfort it would be worthwhile.

Sage Hedgehog was even more morose than the fox. The wasted opportunity of the Assembly had depressed him utterly. There was now, it seemed, no hope of alerting the stubborn and feckless Farthing Wood animals to their plight. Then, as he chewed monotonously on a long worm, thinking dire thoughts, Stout Fox appeared to interrupt his reverie.

'Old prophet hedgehog, I beg you to help,' the fox blurted out. 'If you know anything about the otters' methods in curing sickness, tell me.'

Sage Hedgehog paused in his meal. 'Your mate is worse?'

'Day by day.'

'I am sorry for that. Truly. But I fear you are too late to save her. You've brought this misery on yourselves, for there is now no one who has the secret. The otters kept it to themselves.'

Stout Fox sat on his haunches in despair. 'Is there nothing I can do?' he asked.

'Do you know where the otters went after you foxes drove them from here?'

'No.'

'They're probably widely scattered by this time. But if you could find them – any of them – and persuade them to return, that would be your salvation.' The old hedgehog suddenly perked up, as though there might just be a glimmer of hope. 'Indeed,' he resumed in a stronger voice, 'you *must* find them. For the otters are the salvation of all of us and the Wood itself.'

Stout Fox was encouraged. He looked more resolute. 'You're right! Only they can halt the humans' progress. I realize that now. I'll go and search for them and, if I can, I'll take others to help in the search. I won't rest until I find them!' He turned and ran back towards his earth. He would need to find food enough for his vixen to last her until his return.

Stout Vixen received his news without enthusiasm. 'It's useless,' she muttered. 'You'll never locate the otters. I shall be dead in a few days. Nothing can prevent that.'

But the big fox wouldn't be put off. 'I think you're wrong. And it would be contemptible not to try. I'll fetch food for you before I leave. Promise me you'll try to hold on.'

'Very well,' she whispered. 'You have my word.'

Once he had ensured that the vixen had managed to eat at least some of the titbits he had fetched for her, Stout Fox set off to recruit some helpers. He had no close associates and wondered where to begin. He decided that any swift-footed animal with the keen senses of a hunter would be useful in the search. Lightning Weasel dashed across his path.

'Stop!' the fox cried. 'Wait!'

The weasel turned and looked at the larger animal curiously. 'Well? What is it?' Stout Fox trotted over.

'That's near enough, if you don't want me to run,' Lightning Weasel said sharply. A fox was not a beast he wanted too close to him. 'I don't believe the badger's Oath thing is still in force?'

Stout Fox blinked. 'Oath? What oath?' His mind was on other things. Then he remembered.

'Oh, that. I think not. I want to ask for your help.'

'Help? From me?' the weasel queried in astonishment.

'Yes, I'm going to look for the otters. You see, I need their knowledge to save my mate.'

'Oh, the sickness. Yes, we heard all about that at the Assembly. But this is a bit rich. You drove the otters away and now you want me to help you bring them back. That's your problem, I think.'

'I know it sounds odd. I regret now what we foxes did. We all need them here. Without them what future is there for Farthing Wood?'

'Too late for regrets, I'm afraid. No, count me out. I've no time to waste on a fool's errand and, besides, you're no friend to me, so why should I help?'

'But surely, you know how I feel,' Stout Fox said dejectedly. 'Your own mate died of the sickness.'

'That's right. And now I have another mate. If yours dies, you'll soon find another too. That's Nature, isn't it?' Lightning Weasel wasn't prepared to listen any further and bolted into the undergrowth.

Stout Fox sighed and continued on his errand. He began to realize that there wouldn't be much help forthcoming except from other foxes. He did approach Sly Stoat but there was no sympathy from that quarter either.

'*I* don't want the otters back. They took our food from our mouths. When we laid the trail of disease for them, I couldn't have foreseen how I would be repaid in kind. Now you're reaping the same reward. The otters have avenged themselves on us and there's no escaping it.'

Stout Fox accepted that he must look for assistance from his own kind. But he was no luckier with other foxes. These animals, the very ones who had combined to drive out the otter population, scoffed at the notion of inviting them back.

'You're mad,' one said. 'If we'd wanted them here in the first place, they'd still be around.'

'Though *we* might not be,' added another, 'the way our food was being thieved.'

'We're sorry for your mate,' Lean Vixen told him. 'She could have exercised more caution. But you really can't expect us to fight your battles for you.'

'He's only asking for a little help in his search,' Lean Fox reminded her, as usual the more sympathetic listener. 'I could perhaps go with him for a while.'

'And leave me to fend alone for our cubs?' the vixen retorted. 'Don't even consider it!'

'No, no, she's right,' Stout Fox murmured, bowing to the inevitable. 'I shall go alone. I was wrong to try to involve others in my difficulties.'

When he was out of earshot Lean Vixen growled, 'And woe betide any otters he manages to round up. Because they'll find a funny sort of welcome awaiting them in Farthing Wood.'

Long-Whiskers awoke at the end of the night. Rain was falling heavily and she felt cold. She heaved herself further under the hedgerow. Her coat was thoroughly damp but the raindrops helped to revive her. As dawn broke she became aware of the movements of birds. There were nests along that hedgerow and the parent birds, at first light, resumed their quest for food for the nestlings. Long-Whiskers watched them flying to and fro, and she was able to locate the various nests by the twittering of the hungry chicks, and also by the places where the adults entered and left the hedge. Despite her painful wounds, Long-Whiskers felt hungry. She began to raid those nests within reach, one by one. The young birds stood no chance. Their parents cried their distress as they saw the hunter in the hedgerow, knowing they were powerless to intervene.

In the daylight Long-Whiskers licked her chops as she rested again out of sight. She had a full stomach and already she felt stronger.

Under cover of darkness Stout Fox paddled across the stream and skirted the remaining grassland. He knew the otters would have first crossed the grassland to escape the angry foxes' pursuit. The building works loomed ominously in the distance. All was quiet, but the fox smelt human smells and the unfamiliar odours of their machines and materials hanging on the air. Above all there was the stench of mud. He saw a rabbit skip across the fringe of the muddy area and then disappear underground. He was surprised by just how close the rabbits' burrows were to the human presence. The grassland had been inhabited by rabbits and hares for as long as any animal in Farthing Wood could remember. Now some of that area had been destroyed and they had had to move their homes into the Wood.

Thus they were more vulnerable to marauding foxes, stoats and weasels.

Stout Fox steered clear of the parts changed by the humans. He discovered that this area extended farther than he and probably any other creature had realized. No animal, save the rabbits, had ventured anywhere near it. He thought it his duty to describe to those who would listen what he had seen.

'But that must come later,' he told himself. 'First I have to sniff out the hiding-place of those clever otters.'

16. A Morass

THE HARES and most of the rabbits had indeed migrated into Farthing Wood itself. But, in addition to the added danger of their being within easier reach of their habitual predators, there was pressure for space. A single warren remained in use outside the Wood. It was one of the rabbits from here that Stout Fox had noticed. There were many young – some still suckling – living in the network of tunnels. The rabbits, though fearful of the human din, had almost grown used to the noise and alarms created every day by the builders and their machines. By day they cowered quietly in their burrows. None went above ground until each last sound made by the humans had died away. And even then they waited and waited, finally peeping out to see if it was safe to browse. Usually one of them gave the all-clear signal and then the adults and adolescents would gladly run free and begin to feed.

A period of rain followed Stout Fox's departure. The area around the warren became increasingly muddy. The burrow entrances and the tunnels seeped with mud and the rabbits were very miserable. They wished they had been able to move home. But the babies couldn't yet be moved.

The rain didn't, of course, prevent the humans from proceeding with their affairs. And, to the unfortunate rabbits, it seemed as though the noise and bustle was coming perilously close. They squatted in their slimy tunnels and passages, ears pricked and noses permanently a-quiver. Outside a bulldozer roared and slithered, teetering on one side, then the other, as its angle was dictated by the unstable mud. All at once daylight flooded into the warren. The bulldozer had carved out a huge mass of soil, ripping into one edge of the warren itself. The rabbits fled into the deeper heart of the system. But they were not safe. The bulldozer, having dumped its latest load, reversed and trundled forward again like a juggernaut. Nothing could divert it. Its course was set. The warren was in its path.

As if opening its jaws for another mighty bite, the machine ploughed into the centre of the warren, tearing up the entire labyrinth of runs, nesting burrows with its nursing mothers, babies, and most of the other fugitive rabbits. The load was hoisted high. Rabbits leapt or fell to the ground in terror. Others dangled from the mud, half in and half out of a mangled run. The bulldozer swung round, tipping more animals out as it turned, then depositing the remainder in a pile of soil and sludge where they squirmed like so many worms. They were trapped by the impacted mud and couldn't wriggle clear.

By this time cries from other workers on the site had alerted the earth-mover's driver to what had happened. He quickly turned off his engine as he saw the rabbits struggling and thrashing in the morass, while others twitched helplessly on the ground where they had been flung or had fallen. Only a few animals managed to escape unharmed. A look of consternation passed across the face of the driver who had quite unwittingly caused the destruction of the warren. He jumped from his cab. Other men squelched through the mud to try to free the half-buried animals. When they found the babies, some still beneath their mothers' bodies, they called out to each other in mutual pity and compassion. The driver looked particularly upset. The men did what they could for the animals who had survived, clumsily trying to clean them up and then setting them free. The few rabbits who were unhurt bounded into the Wood.

There was now a kind of bank of mud and grass remaining where the greedy jaws of the earth-mover hadn't yet reached. Inside this bank the last remnants of the rabbits from the warren hid in the few vestiges of holes and passages the machine had missed. They waited, passive victims, for the monster to gobble them up. They were exposed; cut off from any further retreat. There was nowhere to run. Yet somehow they seemed to be forgotten. They didn't hear the roar of the machine that they expected to hear. And they were left, to their amazement, undisturbed. The humans, strangely affected by what had recently happened, left that part of the site alone for the rest of the day and began working elsewhere.

Rain continued to fall. The treacherous mud absorbed more and more water until it was saturated. Puddles formed on its surface. The bank, too, was saturated through and gouts of mud broke away from it and slid down its side. The ground there was very unstable. Cold, wet and frightened, the rabbits inside the bank shivered through the day in a huddle. When darkness brought a cessation of human activity, one danger was replaced by another. The exposed holes in the bank were an open invitation to any hunter who picked up the rabbits' scent.

The foxes, of course, did so. There were more rabbits in the Wood, trying to enter other families' burrows and dens after fleeing the humans. Some were accepted, but in other places there was overcrowding already. The foxes went on a killing spree. Stoats and weasels joined in. A number of rabbits, driven from one side to the other in their efforts to escape, even began to run back to the muddy building site which had recently been their home. A few predators pursued them. Amongst these were Lean Fox and Lean Vixen.

'The cubs must do without their mother for a while,' the vixen had told her mate. 'I shall eat rabbit tonight, and I don't mean to be left out of the chase.'

Lean Fox knew better than to gainsay her. The two ran together. They started an adult rabbit on the fringe of the Wood and raced in pursuit. Another rabbit ran from their approach. Lean Fox chose this one, the vixen the other. It was soon apparent that these rabbits had no bolt-holes. They dashed out of the Wood and on to the top of the bank.

'Catch it, catch it,' Lean Vixen called to her mate as she hurtled after her own quarry.

The rabbits hesitated. The foxes' hot breath ruffled their fur. They leapt and landed in the sticky morass of mud where so many of their own kind had already met their fate. Lean Fox had no time to draw back. He crashed after them, the weight of his body embedding him in the ooze. He saw Lean Vixen falter on the brink.

'Don't jump!' he cried. 'It's a trap!'

Lean Vixen watched her mate thrashing about in his attempts to free himself from the quagmire. She saw the rabbits – their prey – beginning to pull their lighter bodies out of the mud. The rain beat down on them all mercilessly.

'They're getting away!' Lean Vixen shrilled, her one concern above all else being the loss of her prize. Lean Fox struggled harder, but the cloying mud seemed to engulf his body. Lean Vixen teetered indecisively. Suddenly beneath her feet she spied another rabbit trembling in its inadequate hole. Instinctively she began to dig, more and more furiously as the urge to kill enveloped her. The hole gaped and crumbled and, as she lunged, the entire bank collapsed, burying her mate and the fleeing rabbits, while she was brought crashing down with it. Where the bank broke, a rush of water from the swollen stream flooded through the breach, and Lean Vixen was swamped by more mud, carried by the spate. The water poured over her head and the few rabbits who had been sheltering in the unstable bank were drowned with her. Some small trees, whose roots were ripped out of the soil by the subsidence, fell on their sides. The breach, blocked by tree-trunks, vegetation and gathering silt, was sealed. But a new muddy pond had formed on the edge of the building site. On its surface two dead foxes and a number of rabbits floated: a testimony to the human menace. The first animals had been killed, the first trees had been felled. Moreover a small, but ominous, gap had appeared like an open wound in Farthing Wood.

Beyond this place of drama Long-Whiskers was ready to continue her return journey. It was dark. The rain beat against the hedgerow with a relentless rhythm. She shook her coat vigorously and set off. Recognizable features that she passed on her way cheered her and strengthened her determination. Traffic noise reminded her of the road she must cross eventually. 'It won't be so formidable now I'm alone,' she said to herself, thinking of Lame Otter's vulnerability. But at once her thoughts were full of her own solitariness and she felt forlorn.

'You are my companions,' she whispered to her unborn cubs. 'Though I travel alone, we travel together.'

She stopped just short of the road, hiding in a leafy garden. Her sores were healing and she was almost able to put them out of her mind.

From the opposite direction Stout Fox set his face against the lash of the rain. The taint of otter tracks was still strong enough for his sensitive nose to detect. He was pleased with his progress. His ailing vixen was constantly on his mind. He knew time was not on her side. He pictured her, head on paws, lying morosely in their den.

'I must save her. I *will* save her.' Stout Fox kept up this chant as he went, urging himself on to a greater effort and pace. 'The otters have the secret, and I have their scent.'

In the morning Nervous Squirrel saw the devastation. 'A hole! A hole in Farthing Wood!'

And Jay screamed, 'Dead foxes! Dead rabbits! Who's next? Who's next?'

17. Fear and Regret

THE DEATHS of Lean Fox and Lean Vixen, as well as the way Farthing Wood had been penetrated, soon became common knowledge. While the humans busied themselves with cleaning up operations, news of their advance, slight though it was, spread through the Wood like a flame.

'I told you, I warned you,' Sage Hedgehog cried bitterly to anyone who would listen. And now most did. 'They intend to destroy us. Little by little, Farthing Wood will fall. We're in their grasp and they won't let go. Only the otters held the key to our preservation. And where are they now?'

'Stout Fox is searching for them,' Sly Stoat said. 'Oh, how I regret I didn't go with him!'

'It's never too late,' Kindly Badger said. 'He needs help. He asked for it and was rejected. And the Wood is at the mercy of the humans if he fails. We have a duty to go. We can't depend on one creature alone for our salvation.'

'Were I young I'd be with the fox now,' Sage Hedgehog said sadly. 'But, as I'm constantly reminded, I'm old and forgetful of the ways of the young.'

'You have more than played your part already,' Kindly Badger assured him. 'If we had listened more to you at the beginning, things might have been very different.' He turned to Sly Stoat. 'There's no time left for talking. We should bring all the animals together who want to help save Farthing

Wood, and leave this very night. If the otters are still around, one of us should be able to discover them.'

There was quite a gathering that crept carefully from the Wood in the dead of night and dispersed beyond the humans' workings in the all-important search. Stout Vixen had tottered to the earth entrance to watch the departure. It was impossible for her not to know what was afoot. Murmurs, rumours and chatter had been audible above ground for hours. She wondered how far her mate had travelled and whether he had met with any success. She was battling to fight off the sinister clutches of the disease – forcing herself to eat, lapping at raindrops, and determined to 'hold on' for Stout Fox's return as she had promised him.

Long-Whiskers awoke in the garden. A loud clatter outside the house disturbed her. At once she tensed, her muscles taut and ready to power her into flight. There was nothing to be seen, but she sensed a presence. Whatever it was, it wasn't human and she relaxed a fraction. A feeling of weariness overcame her. She had over-exerted herself the previous night and was reminded now of her weak state. She must lie low and conserve her strength for a while. She thought of her abandoned holt. How long ago it seemed when she and the other otters had played so freely and carelessly in the snow! And how ill-deserved was their fate at the hands of the foxes. She thought of them with hatred. The misery she and the others had suffered, the futility of their escape from Farthing Wood, the accidents, the deaths – all as a result of the foxes' jealousy and persecution.

Long-Whiskers lay down again amongst the drenched plants in the garden. She didn't feel ready to eat yet and wanted only to rest. Then all at once she saw the creature who had caused the clatter. It was a fox.

The fox was a well-built animal. It had smelt meat outside the house and had overturned a dustbin to get at it. It was making a meal from human left-overs. Long-Whiskers' heart beat fast. She recognized the animal at once as Stout Fox, the most powerful of the foxes from Farthing Wood. She shrank back, unsure whether to remain or run. What was the fox doing there? Why had it left the Wood? The conclusion she reached was one that made her shudder. It was hunting for her!

Naturally Long-Whiskers knew nothing of the change of heart regarding the otters in Farthing Wood. She remembered only the animosity and the savagery of the foxes. She believed now that Stout Fox had come to seek out every otter; to ensure that the last of them was killed so that there could never be any recurrence of the rivalry over food. And she suspected also that there were others of his kind around, bent on the same task. She was in terrible danger. She thought of her cubs. She must preserve their chance of survival at all costs. She knew all about the foxes' powerful senses of smell and hearing. She didn't think she could avoid discovery in the garden.

Slowly, painfully slowly, Long-Whiskers pulled herself from the vegetation and began to move off. A flicker of movement might have given her away, but the fox's head was turned towards the house. Long-Whiskers increased her speed. Now the rustle of her body made Stout Fox look round. He sniffed the air. He saw where the plants waved and parted. He ran forward. Long-Whiskers could think only of escape. She broke into a run and headed for the road. It was not late and there was traffic passing at intervals. With the fox behind her, the otter had to gamble. To be caught by the fox she believed would mean certain death. As for the human machines, there was just a possibility she could dodge them.

Stout Fox saw her intention. 'Don't run from me!' he barked. 'You don't understand: I haven't come to harm you. I've come for your help.'

Long-Whiskers was oblivious to his cries. She was concentrating as hard as she could on choosing her moment. She saw that the swift machines had separate movements. There were spaces between their passing. But she had no idea of their speed. To an animal it was unimaginable.

'Stop!' the fox barked. He could see her desperation. 'You'll be killed! The machines. They –' His last bark was muffled by the roar of a huge lorry. When it had passed, Long-Whiskers had disappeared. She was neither on his side of the road, nor across on the other. He sniffed the air for her scent. It was there. He looked down the road. And then he saw her. One of the giant wheels of the lorry had struck Long-Whiskers a glancing blow, sending her spinning through the air. She had landed some metres away, farther up the road, and was trying to drag herself from its surface.

'She's injured,' Stout Fox muttered. 'Her legs are crushed. I must try to pull her free.'

Traffic continued to pass. No vehicle stopped, but each one went around the struggling otter. Stout Fox trotted forward. Selfishly, he had no thought at that moment of the otter's vital importance to Farthing Wood. His one idea was to obtain the information he needed for his vixen's survival. As soon as it was safe, he crossed the road.

Long-Whiskers saw him approaching. She knew she had no defences. 'So you've come to finish me off?' she gasped. The fox ignored her. He grasped her by the nape of the neck and lifted her in his jaws. She was heavy. He laid her in soft grass in the nearest field. She stared up at him with glassy eyes.

'The machine has done the job you came to do,' she panted.

Stout Fox blinked uncomprehendingly. 'Where are the others?' he asked.

Long-Whiskers sighed a long sigh. 'There *are* no others. I'm the last. And in me die the last of the Farthing Wood otters.'

'But you mustn't die. Not yet,' Stout Fox pleaded. 'You saved yourself from the sickness. Give me the knowledge, I beg you, to save my mate.'

A realization seemed to dawn in Long-Whiskers' eyes. 'So that's why you came?' she whispered.

Much distressed, Stout Fox recalled his other motivation. 'No, not that alone. I came to find you and to bring you home. Our home. The home we all share.'

'Ha! There'll be no home for me,' Long-Whiskers answered him with bitterness. 'And neither for my cubs.'

'You have cubs?' Stout Fox exclaimed. 'Then you're not the last.'

'My cubs die with me.'

The fox understood and, remembering all that had passed, a great sadness overcame him. He knew the foxes bore the blame for the present situation. 'Forgive us for bringing you to this plight,' he muttered brokenly.

Long-Whiskers didn't reply.

'I would like to help you if I can,' the fox resumed.

'I'm beyond help.'

'Perhaps not. Farthing Wood is close. We need you.'

'Oh yes,' the otter gasped with the irony. 'For giving you my knowledge. Ha! When we lived together, foxes and otters, you didn't want our knowledge. Only our extinction.'

This was horribly true and Stout Fox had no reply to give.

'Why should I, then, help *you*?' Long-Whiskers demanded.

'I have no right to ask.'

'Your mate is sick? What kind of sickness?'

Stout Fox explained.

Long-Whiskers was silent for a long while. Then she murmured, 'There is no help I can give you, even if I would. I was not one of the otters who fell sick from disease. It's true some of us who were sick were able to heal themselves. I don't know how.'

'You – you have no idea?' Stout Fox asked hopelessly.

'Perhaps a plant . . . I can't say . . . ' The otter's head drooped. She seemed about to expire.

'Please, what can I do for you?' the fox beseeched her earnestly.

Several moments passed. The otter rallied. 'As we're . . . no longer enemies,' she said weakly, 'maybe you could stay with me until . . . ' She left the rest unsaid; it wasn't necessary to finish.

Stout Fox was in a dilemma. He greatly wished to make recompense for the tragedy he had brought about. On the other hand time was running out for his vixen and he was desperate to get back to her. The otter bitch looked as if she couldn't last much longer. He tried to be patient. 'I'll wait with you,' he said softly.

Some of the other animals who were searching – the swiftest runners – had covered a lot of ground in very little time. Lightning Weasel was the fastest of these. He detected the musky odour of fox. He looked around. He saw Stout Fox lying, nose to tail, a little way ahead. Was he asleep? The weasel crept forward. He saw that there was another animal by the fox's side.

Stout Fox opened one eye. 'You have nothing to fear from me,' he said. 'I'm not hunting, although *you* clearly are. Why have you come so far?'

'To look for the otters,' Lightning Weasel squeaked.

Stout Fox's ears pricked. 'Then your search is at an end,' he said.

The weasel began to understand. 'You – you have found one?'

'Come nearer.'

Lightning Weasel trotted up. 'Is the otter dead?'

'Not quite. And why are you searching now? You didn't want to come with me when I asked you.'

The weasel explained about the hole in Farthing Wood, the dead foxes and the rabbits.

Stout Fox sat bolt upright. 'Which foxes were killed?' he demanded.

The weasel told him. Stout Fox sank back. 'Well, you and the other beasts and myself, too – we're all too late. The otters have been wiped out. I tried to save this one here, but failed. She told me she's the last. When she dies perhaps Farthing Wood will begin to die too.'

Lightning Weasel sniffed at Long-Whiskers. She was quite still and, seeing this, the weasel for once became still too. He and Stout Fox waited together quietly and, later, other animals found their way to the spot. Sly Stoat and Kindly Badger were among them. Together they waited in silence as though doing penance for the demise of the Farthing Wood otters.

18. The Otters' Secret

BEFORE dawn all the animals were on their way home. Subdued and downhearted, they drifted back in ones and twos to their dens and burrows. The significance of Long-Whiskers' death weighed heavily on all of them.

As light began to fill the sky, Stout Fox headed for the stream in a last effort to unlock the secret of the otters' knowledge. He felt that somewhere along the water's edge where they had chosen their holts, there might be a clue waiting to be discovered. He cast his eyes along the bank and around the territory. Then he swam the stream and did the same on the side bordering the Wood. He stared at each plant, trying to assess its value and hoping for enlightenment. Nothing struck him as being unusual.

'Oh, those otters,' he moaned to himself. 'Even now they're dead and gone they still haunt me. How was it they were able to do things we other animals can't? What made them so different?' He ran along the bank, shaking his head. All at once an idea came into his mind. 'There was one thing that made them different from us,' he murmured. 'Their love of water, their wonderful skill in diving and swimming. Perhaps there's something in the water that's beneficial . . .' He bent and lapped experimentally, but there was nothing to taste then, any more than the hundreds of other times he had drunk from it.

'I hate to return to the vixen with no hope,' he muttered. 'But I mustn't leave her any longer. I've tried to find the cure. I've done all I can.'

He ran on into the Wood, eager to see Stout Vixen again, yet dreading to find her worse than before. He came upon her asleep in their earth. He was loth to wake her, but she sensed his company.

'You're back then,' she whispered. 'I – I managed to hold on.'

'You look so weak . . . '

'Did you learn anything?' she asked with a glimmer of hope.

Stout Fox looked down. 'The otters are all dead. Their secret died with them.'

The vixen heaved a long sigh as if finally she was letting go. But Stout Fox said quickly, 'Listen. Can you walk? I want you to come to the stream. Try to drink some water. It may do some good.'

'What's the point?' she asked him hoarsely. 'I might as well die here as there.'

'There's just a chance. Please – for me and our cubs.'

'Our cubs will never be born.'

'You mustn't say that! You *must* try.'

Wearily, painfully, the vixen got to her feet. Stout Fox nuzzled her and nudged her to the entrance hole. She swayed, unused to any kind of exertion. Patiently and with sympathy he encouraged her to walk. For the vixen, it seemed each step was more difficult than the last.

The edge of the Wood was a long way off. They paused often to allow her to rest. The noise of machinery echoed through the woodland, emphasizing the peril that each creature now recognized was its inheritance. Even Jay's screeches of alarm were drowned by the brutality of the bulldozers. Stout Fox had no need to explain the state of affairs to his mate. She knew enough to realize that, if ever their cubs were born, they would be born into a hostile world.

*

Somehow Stout Vixen got herself to the fringes of Farthing Wood. By then it was growing dark again. She gasped, 'Where is the nearest water? My legs won't take me any farther.'

'Here. Just over here,' the fox called. The rain at last had ceased and the pale moon was reflected in the dark swollen stream.

The vixen crawled on her belly to the bank and let her muzzle drop into the water.

'There's a lot of growth there.' Stout Fox pointed out a mass of cressy plants tangled underwater. 'Come to where I'm standing. The stream runs clearer here.'

Stout Vixen raised her head. Strands of the plants were draped over her muzzle. 'Growth or no growth,' she panted, 'this is where I stop.' She bent and drank greedily. The water was cold and, while drinking it, she swallowed some cress. She sucked in a good mouthful of the plant and chewed it, relishing its clean peppery taste. Then she lay her head on her paws and fell asleep where she was.

Later the vixen awoke and noticed at once that the dull ache in the pit of her stomach which had troubled her for so long had disappeared. She felt less listless than she had done for many days. She looked up. Stout Fox was absent. She scrambled to her feet, still weak but tremendously hungry. As she savoured her new feeling of well-being her mate came trotting from the Wood. A dead rabbit dangled from his jaws. He had scarcely dropped it before Stout Vixen seized it ravenously and began to tear off mouthfuls.

'Well, this is a transformation,' the fox commented delightedly. 'The water, then, has been of some help.'

'I think it was the plant,' Stout Vixen mumbled, her mouth full. 'It's purged me.'

'The plant?' Stout Fox whispered, recalling Long-Whiskers' words. 'So that's it! Yes,' he cried, 'of course. That's how the otters were healed. Waterplants!' He peered into the stream. 'Will you take some more?' he asked eagerly.

'Certainly,' the vixen replied. 'I intend to make a full recovery. I shall need to build up my strength again quickly.'

'The cubs!'

'Yes. You have been a good mate. You made me struggle here almost against my will. The stream did hold the clue and you were right to insist.'

Stout Fox was jubilant. He had saved his vixen and, in that joyful knowledge, the fate of Farthing Wood was for a while forgotten.

Two days later Stout Vixen gave birth to four cubs. The poison that had infected her caused three of them to be still-born. The fourth, a male cub, by way of compensation looked to be robust. Stout Vixen removed the rest of her litter from the earth with resignation.

'One little cub to face an uncertain future,' Stout Fox murmured sadly.

'But a future with some hope if he has your wits,' Stout Vixen remarked.

Epilogue

AS THE little animal grew, the building works took shape. Most of the grassland was swallowed up. Life in Farthing Wood continued as always. There were births and deaths, fights and quarrels. Prey was hunted, homes were excavated. There was nowhere else for the inhabitants of the Wood to go.

One day a large tree was felled. It toppled with a terrifying crash that seemed to shake the Wood to its foundations. In the eerie stillness that followed one creature, the old hedgehog, thought he heard again the mocking taunts of the otters.

'Well, Farthing Wood, we hope you like your neighbours! You didn't want us here, but look who came instead. We were your surety. Without us you are lost. Who will save you now?'

Sage Hedgehog stared into the distance as though looking beyond his surroundings and the present time to something that was yet to happen. 'A leader will come along,' he said, answering those ghostly voices with a sudden conviction. 'Everyone will unite to follow him. And *that's* how we shall be saved.'

COLIN DANN

1943	*Born on 10 March in Richmond, Surrey*
1966	*Begins his career at the publishing house, William Collins, Sons & Co.*
1978	*Stops working at William Collins, Sons & Co to become a full-time writer*
1979	The Animals of Farthing Wood *is published by John Goodchild publishers*
1980	The Animals of Farthing Wood *wins the Arts Council National Award for Children's Literature*
1981	In the Grip of Winter, *the second novel in The Animals of Farthing Wood series, is published*
1982	Fox's Feud, *the third novel in the series, is published*
1983	The Fox Cub Bold, *the fourth novel in the series, is published*
1985	The Siege of White Deer Park, *the fifth novel in the series, is published*

1989	In the Path of the Storm, *the sixth novel in the series, is published*
1992	Battle for the Park, *the final story in the series, is published*
1993	The Animals of Farthing Wood *is adapted for a children's television series and is first aired in Germany, Belgium, Ireland and the United Kingdom, followed a little later by France*
1994	The Adventure Begins, *the prequel to The Animals of Farthing Wood series, is published*

INTERESTING FACTS

The Animals of Farthing Wood was translated into sixteen languages.

It was first printed for a children's book club as two separate paperbacks titled *Escape from Danger* and *The Way to White Deer Park*. All subsequent editions were printed as one complete story.

The Animals of Farthing Wood TV series cost £6 million pounds to make, and was viewed by an estimated sixty million people across Europe when it was first aired.

WHERE DID THE
STORY COME FROM?

*Colin Dann says: 'When the TV series was due to be aired,
my editor at that time suggested a prequel to* The Animals
of Farthing Wood. *I thought this was a good idea. There
were references in* The Animals of Farthing Wood *to earlier
events, such as the Oath of Common Safety, when the
wood's inhabitants gathered to discuss the threat to their
livelihoods. So in the prequel I was able to show how that
meeting was inconclusive, but could be viewed as a kind
of omen of the more important meeting a generation on,
when the animals finally bonded and agreed to flee. The
other factor – the sudden arrival of human developers –
needed to be explained too. The disappearance of the
otters was crucial to that and set it in motion. I wanted the
visionary Sage Hedgehog to warn the animals about this
and the dangers to come and, though he was ignored, for
him to retain the conviction that, by working together, they
would eventually find their salvation.*

GUESS WHO?

A *'The mice are here for any hunter to catch. It's not my fault you weren't skilful enough to catch them first.'*

B *'We don't want human intruders around when our cubs are born.'*

C *'You were wrong to make war with the otters,' he told the foxes. 'You will rue the day you drove them out.'*

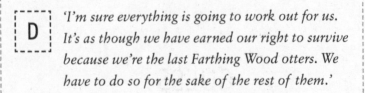

D 'I'm sure everything is going to work out for us. It's as though we have earned our right to survive because we're the last Farthing Wood otters. We have to do so for the sake of the rest of them.'

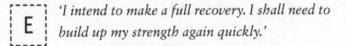

E 'I intend to make a full recovery. I shall need to build up my strength again quickly.'

WORDS GLORIOUS WORDS!

Lots of words have several different meanings – here are a few you'll find in this Puffin book. Use a *dictionary* or look them up online to find other definitions.

holt   *an otter's nest*

conservation   *the protection of wildlife or objects of interest and historical value*

eerie   *mysterious, frightening or disturbing*

resolute   *to be determined to do something*

spate   *when a river has more water than usual and is flowing very fast*

penance   *an act that shows sorrow or a feeling of regret for something you have done*

QUIZ

1 *When the otters get ill, what do they eat to make themselves better?*

a) *Grass*

b) *Bark*

c) *A water plant*

d) *A fish*

2 *When the otters are playing in the stream, who comes to watch them?*

a) *Nervous Squirrel*

b) *Kindly Badger*

c) *Lean Fox*

d) *Humans*

3 *Why was Slow Otter jealous of Lame Otter?*

a) *Because Lame Otter was better at hunting than Slow Otter*

b) *Because Lame Otter was faster than Slow Otter*

c) *Because Lame Otter was more popular with the female otters than Slow Otter*

d) *Because Lame Otter had a better holt than Slow Otter*

4 *Why did Sage Hedgehog like being near Farthing Pond?*

a) *He liked to swim*

b) *His favourite food, snails and snugs, could be found there*

c) *His best friend, Kindly Badger, lived near there*

d) *He could hide easily in the vegetation around the pond*

5 *Why did the senior animals in the wood meet at the Great Beech?*

a) *Because the humans were building a new road so they needed to plan how they would survive*

b) *They wanted to see if they could climb up it to use it as a look out*

c) *Because the humans were coming to catch them*

d) *To share a meal of voles*

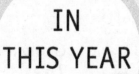

IN
THIS YEAR

1994
Fact Pack

*What else was
happening in the
world when this story
was first published?*

COLIN DANN
THE ANIMALS OF
FARTHING WOOD
THE ADVENTURE BEGINS

The **World Wide Web** is born – *now known as
the internet.*

The film **The Lion King** *is released and
becomes an instant Disney classic.*

The Channel Tunnel *is opened between
England and France.*

The Sony **PlayStation** *is launched.*

Nelson Mandela *becomes President of South
Africa.*

MAKE AND DO

Grow a Tree!

If you care about forests and jungles, and the wildlife that lives in them, then you can start your own conservation project at home by planting your first tree. It's easier than you might think . . .

YOU WILL NEED:

* A plant pot or a plastic container with holes in the bottom
* Gardening gloves
* Small stones or grit
* Soil
* Compost
* Some tree seeds
* A little water

1 Go for a walk in a park with your parent or guardian and collect some seeds. You could try a conker from a horse chestnut tree, acorns from an oak tree or helicopter seeds from a sycamore tree, or all three!

2 Check that your seeds look healthy and don't have any bugs in them.

3 Put grit or a few small stones into the bottom of your container to help with drainage.

4 Add a bit of soil and compost – about two centimetres deep.

5 Place your seeds on top of the soil, and then fill the rest of the container up to the top with more soil and compost.

6 Give your pot some water, but not too much.

7 Place your pot in a shady spot outside. It's best to plant your seed in autumn so it can get really cold in winter. The cold will help your seed germinate and sprout in the springtime.

8 *Check your pot every few weeks to make sure it's not too dry. If it is, then give it a little more water.*

9 *Wait until spring to see if your seed has sprouted a shoot. It is a good idea to plant more than one pot to increase your chances of growing a healthy tree.*

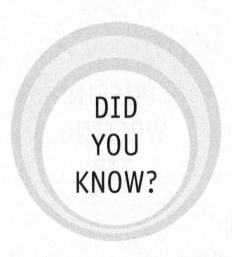

DID
YOU
KNOW?

Otters have very sensitive paws to help them find shellfish in the mud at the bottom of rivers.

Foxes have whiskers on their legs as well as around their faces, which they use to help them find their way.

A hedgehog has about five thousand prickly spines, which they use to protect themselves against predators.

Squirrels sometimes pretend to bury food to trick potential thieves!

Owls can turn their heads up to 270 degrees. This is useful because they can't move their eyeballs around.

PUFFIN WRITING TIP

Practise writing every day by keeping a **diary**.

At the end of the month, **read back** through your diary and **edit** out the boring bits.

If you're really brave, **share** your diary with your parents or guardian for **feedback!**

If you have enjoyed this book, you may like to read *Mrs Frisby and the Rats of NIMH* by Robert C. O'Brien in which Mrs Frisby struggles to protect her family of mice and receives some unexpected help from a group of highly intelligent rats . . .

11. In the Library

THE TUNNEL led gently downwards, and after the first dozen steps they were in darkness. Mrs Frisby could see nothing at all. Behind her Mr Ages limped along; ahead she could hear the scuffle of Justin's footsteps. She followed the sound blindly. Then she heard his voice.

'Just walk straight forward, Mrs Frisby. There's nothing to trip over, and nothing to bump into. If you get off course, you'll feel the wall.' He added: 'The dark part doesn't last long.'

Now what did he mean by that? She thought it over for a minute or two as she walked and had just decided to ask him, when to her surprise she saw ahead of her a faint glow. A light! But how could there be a light down so far? 'There, we're through it,' said Justin cheerfully. 'I know that blackout bit must be annoying the first time, but it's necessary.'

'But aren't we under the ground?'

'Oh yes. About three feet down by now, I'd guess.'

'Then how can it be light?'

'I could tell you,' Justin said, 'but if you'll wait fifteen seconds, you'll see for yourself.'

In a few more steps the tunnel – Mrs Frisby could now discern, dimly, its shape and direction – took a turn to the right, and she did see for herself. She stopped in astonishment.

Ahead of her stretched a long, well-lit hallway. Its ceiling and walls were a smoothly curved arch, its floor hard and flat, with a soft layer of carpet down the middle. The light came from the walls, where every foot or so on both sides a tiny light bulb had been recessed and the hole in which it stood, like a small window, had been covered with a square of coloured glass – blue, green or yellow. The effect was that of stained-glass windows in sunlight.

Justin was watching her and smiling. 'Do you like it? The carpet and the coloured glass we don't really need. Some of the wives did that on their own, just for looks. They cut the glass, believe it or not, from old bottles. The carpet was a piece of trim they found somewhere.'

'It's beautiful,' Mrs Frisby said. 'But how . . .'

'We've had electricity for years now.'

'Five,' said Mr Ages.

'Five,' said Justin agreeably. 'The lights' – they were the very small, very bright twinkling kind – 'we found on trees. In fact, most of our lights come from trees. Not until after Christmas, of course – about New Year. The big light bulbs we have trouble handling.'

Mrs Frisby was familiar with electricity (her husband, who knew all kinds of things, had once explained it to her). At night she had seen the lamps shining in Mr Fitzgibbon's house, and at Christmas time the lights that his sons strung on a pine tree outside.

'You mean you just took them?' she asked.

'We were careful to take only a few from each tree,' said Mr Ages.

'It was like picking fruit,' Justin said rather dreamily. 'The annual light bulb harvest. We had to go quite far up the road before we had enough. Even so, it took two Christmases.'

'Justin,' said Mr Ages, 'I think we'd better get on.'

They continued along the corridor, which curved always slightly to the right, so Mrs Frisby could never really tell how long it was, and which soon began to incline more steeply into the ground. Mrs Frisby noticed that the air, which should have been dank and damp so deep underground, was on the contrary fresh and clean, and she thought she could even detect a very faint breeze blowing past her ears as she moved.

In a few more minutes the hall widened abruptly into a large oval chamber. Here the lights were set in the ceiling; at the far end, Mrs Frisby could see, the long tunnel continued and looked as if it slanted upward again – perhaps to another entrance, a back door. Was this, then, their destination, the main hall of the rats? But if so, where were all the other rats? The room was entirely empty – not even a stick of furniture.

'A storeroom,' said Justin. 'Sometimes full. Now empty.'

Then she saw that off one side of the chamber there was a stairway leading down, and beside it a small door. Justin led them to the door.

'For freight only,' he said with a grin at Mr Ages. 'But considering your limp, I think we can make an exception. The stairs wouldn't be easy.'

Mrs Frisby looked at the stairway. It went down in a spiral and each step was neatly inlaid with a rectangular piece of slate. She could not tell how far down it led, since after the first turn of the spiral she could see no more, but she had a feeling it was a long way down. As Justin said, it would be hard for Mr Ages.

Justin opened the door. It led into a square room that looked like a cupboard.

'After you,' he said. Mrs Frisby went in, the others followed, and the door swung shut. On the wall were two knobs. Justin pushed one of them, and Mrs Frisby, who had never been in a lift before, gasped and almost fell as she felt the floor suddenly sink beneath her feet. Justin reached out a hand to steady her.

'It's all right,' he said. 'I should have warned you.'

'But we're falling!'

'Not quite. We're going down, but we've got two strong cables and an electric motor holding us.'

Still, Mrs Frisby held her breath during the rest of the descent, until finally the small lift came to a gentle stop and Justin opened the door. Then she breathed again and looked out.

The room before her was at least three times as big as the one they had just left, and corridors radiated from it in as many directions as petals from a daisy. Directly opposite the lift an open arch led into what looked like a still larger room – seemingly some kind of an assembly hall, for it had a raised platform at one end.

And now there were rats. Rats by dozens – standing and talking in groups of twos and threes and fours, rats walking slowly, rats hurrying, rats carrying papers. As Mrs Frisby stepped from the elevator, it became obvious that strangers were a rarity down there, for the hubbub of a dozen conversations stopped abruptly, and all heads turned to look at her. They did not look hostile, nor were they alarmed – since her two companions were familiar to them – but merely curious. Then, as quickly as it had died out, the sound of talking began again, as if the rats were too polite to stand and stare. But one of them, a lean rat with a scarred face, left his group and walked towards them.

'Justin. Mr Ages. And I see we have a guest.' He spoke graciously, with an air of quiet dignity, and Mrs Frisby noticed two more things about him. First, the scar on his face ran across his left eye, and over this eye he wore a black patch, fastened by a cord around his head. Second, he carried a satchel – rather like a handbag – by a strap over his shoulders.

'A guest whose name you will recognize,' said Justin. 'She is Mrs Jonathan Frisby. Mrs Frisby, this is Nicodemus.'

'A name I recognize indeed,' said the rat called Nicodemus. 'Mrs Frisby – are you perhaps aware of this? – your late husband was one of our greatest friends. You are welcome here.'

'Thank you,' said Mrs Frisby, but she was more puzzled than ever. 'In fact, I did not know that you knew my husband. But I'm glad to hear it, because I've come to ask your help.'

'Mrs Frisby has a problem,' said Mr Ages. 'An urgent one.'

'If we can help you, we will,' said Nicodemus.

***Mrs Frisby and the Rats of NIMH* is available in A Puffin Book.**

A PUFFIN BOOK

stories that last a lifetime

Ever wanted a friend who could take you to magical realms, talk to animals or help you survive a shipwreck? Well, you'll find them all in the **A PUFFIN BOOK** collection.

A PUFFIN BOOK will stay with you **forever**. Maybe you'll read it again and again, or perhaps years from now you'll suddenly **remember** the moment it made you **laugh** or **cry** or simply see things **differently**. Adventurers **big** and **small**, rebels out to **change** their world, even a mouse with a **dream** and a spider who can spell – these are the characters who make **stories** that last a **lifetime**.

Whether you love animal tales, war stories or want to know what it was like growing up in a different time and place, the **A PUFFIN BOOK** collection has a story for you – you just need to decide where you want to go next . . .